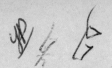

"Did you see that? He was going to kiss her."

Molly pushed her friend Cherish back into the bushes across from Miss Rachel's cabin. She covered her mouth with her hand and held her breath till her dad walked past. Then she exhaled softly.

"Do you think he really was?" Molly stood and danced in place, causing the shrub's leaves to rustle. "That's great. My plan is working! We need to keep them together somehow. Maybe if they go on a date, I'll get to sleep over in your cabin. Wouldn't that be neat. I've never been on a sleepover."

Cherish brushed dirt from her knees, then stared at Molly. "Never?"

"Grandma's house doesn't count. And that's the only other place he lets me sleep."

"That's terrible." Cherish grinned at her friend. "We'll just have to make sure they keep seeing each other. And soon all your dad will be thinking of is Miss Rachel."

"Cool. And then maybe he'll forget about stopping me from having fun."

Dear Reader,

On my seventeenth birthday I got my first driver's license—
and my first organ donor card. I considered it carefully,
spoke to my parents and decided that if something
happened to me and I didn't need those organs anymore,
well, maybe someone else did. I signed the card.

Fast forward twenty years. I was watching television
and came across a show about children having organ
transplants. Bing. A "what if" popped into my mind. What
if a divorced mom who'd lost her only child and donated
his organs fell in love with a single dad whose kid had had
an organ transplant? Rachel, James and Molly were born
out of that "what if."

I spent a lot of time researching. I wept in front of my
computer as I surfed sites that honored child organ donors.
I cried over the kids who needed new hearts but didn't get
them in time. I rejoiced over the kids who did, including
some whose moms "talked" to me about parenting
transplant kids.

But this story isn't just about organ transplant kids. It's
about the power of love to heal and overcome, about the
strength of the human heart in more ways than one. It's
about summer camp and fireflies and rambunctious kids
getting into mischief. It's about a little girl who wants a
new mom to love her.

As always, I'd love to hear from you. Visit my Web site at
www.susangable.com, e-mail me at Susan@susangable.com
or snail mail at P.O. Box 9313, Erie, PA 16505-8313.

May all your firefly wishes come true!

Susan Gable

The Mommy Plan
Susan Gable

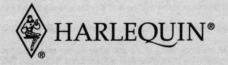

HARLEQUIN®

TORONTO • NEW YORK • LONDON
AMSTERDAM • PARIS • SYDNEY • HAMBURG
STOCKHOLM • ATHENS • TOKYO • MILAN • MADRID
PRAGUE • WARSAW • BUDAPEST • AUCKLAND

ISBN 0-373-71150-6

THE MOMMY PLAN

Copyright © 2003 by Susan Guadagno.

All rights reserved. Except for use in any review, the reproduction or utilization of this work in whole or in part in any form by any electronic, mechanical or other means, now known or hereafter invented, including xerography, photocopying and recording, or in any information storage or retrieval system, is forbidden without the written permission of the publisher, Harlequin Enterprises Limited, 225 Duncan Mill Road, Don Mills, Ontario, Canada M3B 3K9.

All characters in this book have no existence outside the imagination of the author and have no relation whatsoever to anyone bearing the same name or names. They are not even distantly inspired by any individual known or unknown to the author, and all incidents are pure invention.

This edition published by arrangement with Harlequin Books S.A.

® and TM are trademarks of the publisher. Trademarks indicated with ® are registered in the United States Patent and Trademark Office, the Canadian Trade Marks Office and in other countries.

Visit us at www.eHarlequin.com

Printed in U.S.A.

In loving memory of those who left my life
long before I was ready to let them go, and all the
organ donors who have given others a second chance.

ACKNOWLEDGMENTS

As always, thanks to my girls, Kimmy, Lisa and Jen,
who believed in this book so very much.

To Sus, for her proofing skills and support.

To Mona Barmash and CHIN
(Children's Health Information Network—www.tchin.org)
for educating me about congenital heart defects and
hooking me up with other information sources.

To Pat Kornick, from CORE
(Center for Organ Recovery and Education) for answering
my questions about organ donation procedures.

To my "transplant" moms and their inspirational kids,
Mary Rose and Melissa, Dani and Katie,
Shelley and Bryan. I would especially like to thank
Barbara Hochstein and her son, Jon, for giving me
insight into the parenting of a heart transplant child
(James's hang-ups are totally his own)
and answering my million questions
about medications, routines and so on.

CHAPTER ONE

TWO WEEKS.

A two-week stay in this place was supposed to heal the gaping hole in her heart and save her career?

Sure.

If she was lucky, maybe she'd get a Band-Aid out of the deal.

Gravel crunched and popped beneath the tires as Rachel Thompson eased the convertible to a stop. Just ahead, a bright, multicolored sign arced over the dirt road. Camp Firefly Wishes. A place full of miracles, she'd been told.

She could certainly use one of those. But she wouldn't hold her breath.

Her hands trembled, and Rachel gripped the steering wheel harder, turning her knuckles white. If her boss—in cahoots with her father—hadn't insisted, she wouldn't be here, facing something she wasn't certain she'd ever be ready to face.

The hot, mid-July sun made her glad she'd put the top down. The humid air carried the sounds of chirping birds and rustling leaves. She closed her eyes and inhaled deeply, catching the scent of freshly mowed grass.

The smells and sounds of summer vacation. If she tried hard enough, she could make believe that this summer vacation would be the way it always had been: a time of joy and peace, of fireflies, bare feet and children's laughter, of no lesson plans, and time with her family, with her son.

But summer would never be like that again.

A blaring horn jolted her from her reverie. Rachel glanced in the rearview mirror to see a silver SUV practically on her bumper.

The driver offered her a friendly wave, then leaned out his window. "Is anything wrong?"

Rachel shook her head. Anything wrong? More like everything. But somehow she'd get through this.

She eased the GTO into gear and slowly traveled the dirt lane, steering carefully around the potholes still filled with rainwater. On her left, she saw the stables. Several chestnut horses stamped their hooves and nickered as she passed.

A large field—the source of the grassy smell— appeared next. It had the markings of a baseball diamond and a soccer field. All in all, the place looked remarkably like the brochure her principal had forced on her, remarkably like any other summer camp she'd ever attended or seen pictures of— except for the helipad at the far end of the field.

That one detail reminded her this was unlike

those other camps. This one catered to kids who'd had organ transplants and their families. Since the camp was more than an hour's drive north of Pittsburgh, Pennsylvania, the helipad probably reassured parents that competent medical help was only a short flight away. Just in case...

Rachel's throat tightened and she blinked a few times.

A fleeting glance in the mirror showed the SUV still following closely. Which meant a U-turn and quick getaway were out of the question. But escaping wasn't an option, anyway. Rachel had to consider her career. It was all she had left.

The camp's main building—a large, rambling, wood-sided structure—came into view. She chose a parking space near the front doors. The SUV slipped into the slot beside her.

Childish laughter—one of her summer fantasy components—floated to her ears as a family exited the building.

I thought the families weren't arriving until tomorrow? Maybe they weren't campers. Both children appeared robust and energetic as they cavorted along the sidewalk, not at all like what she imagined a transplant child would look like.

Rachel grabbed the leather satchel from the passenger seat and rummaged through its contents. Yanking out the appropriate file, she searched for the letter of confirmation from the camp's owners.

The wind swirled down and lifted the papers into the air.

"Sugar cookies!" She launched herself across the seat after them, managing to land on all but one before they flew away.

A throaty, masculine chuckle made her glance up.

"Such language," the SUV driver gently chided, "yet tempered with grace. I'd give that dive a nine." He offered her the errant sheet of paper. "Here's the one you missed."

Rachel's cheeks warmed, and she straightened up, then ran a hand over her hair as she studied him. A dimple cleaved his angular chin. Short brown hair, the color of rich coffee. Eyes the color of melted caramel. Broad shoulders that tapered down to a narrow waist. He shook the page. "Do you want this back, or should I let the breeze have it, after all?"

Her cheeks flamed hotter as she accepted the paper. "Thanks." She scanned the sheet. "Oh, no." She glanced back at the man who was caressing the top of her passenger door. "What's today?"

"Sunday." He looked down at her. "Nice car."

"Oh no, Sunday? Are you sure?"

"Yes, I'm sure." He extended his hand to her. "I'm James."

"And I'm late!" Rachel stuffed the papers back into the folder. "This isn't happening."

How could she have messed up so badly?

Granted, once school let out for the year, one day seemed the same as the next. But to actually show up on the wrong day?

She really didn't want to be here. Maybe this was her subconscious way of avoiding it. *If your subconscious gets you fired, what then?*

Panic tightened her throat. She shifted across the seat and jumped from the car. "Nice to meet you."

James McClain found himself staring as the woman dashed up the sidewalk. She was thin—almost too thin—but that didn't negate a gently curved and perfectly proportioned rear. Her determined march displayed purpose and a little bit of panic; there was no seductive sashaying, or slinking, and yet he couldn't pull his attention from the seat of her well-fitting white shorts.

"Daddy?"

If ever there was a word designed to burst the bubble of erotic visions, that was it. But then, his girl was worth the sacrifices he made, a normal love life being one of them. Fantasy was about all he could manage. Caring for her and running his psychology practice took all his time.

James turned to face the open window of the SUV and his daughter. "Yeah, tiger?"

"Who was that lady?" Molly, awake from her short nap, leaned out, craning her neck to look around him.

He glanced over his shoulder for a final peek as

the front door swung shut behind the delightful rear.
"I don't know."

"She has pretty hair."

James stifled a chuckle. Therein lay the difference between a thirty-seven-year-old male and an
eight-year-old little girl. Although sometimes his
daughter seemed far older than he was. "Yes, she
does, sweetie. Now, are you ready to camp?"

"I was born ready."

"Whatever you say, Unsinkable."

"Da-a-ad." Molly's eyes narrowed. "You promised not to call me that while we were here. I'm
not a baby anymore."

He stopped himself from telling her she'd always
be his baby. Running a fingertip across her cheek,
he marveled at the healthy pink flush in her skin.
"No, you're not." He pressed gently on her
freckle-covered nose. "But you'll always be the
Unsinkable Molly McClain."

"If I'm so unsinkable, then why don't you let
me do all the things I want to? Like go to camp by
myself?"

Like a normal kid. James heard the qualifier his
daughter left unvoiced. "Molly, you know the reason."

"They do have camps that will take a transplant
kid by themselves, you know. Not like this one,
where the family comes along. Camps that aren't
just about in our own backyard, too."

A thirty-five-minute ride from home wasn't

enough to provide the adventure she craved. "I know. But you're not old enough. Maybe next year." He ignored the prickling sensation at the back of his neck. Planning for next summer seemed incredible, a far cry from last summer—most of which he and Molly had spent at Children's Hospital. With good luck and good management, she'd have a next year. He'd spent a lot of her life praying. And he'd damn near lost her. Her new heart had come just in time. That had been last September—almost a year ago. Her surgeon had worried that she wasn't going to be strong enough to survive the transplant. Now, if he could just keep her new heart healthy...

A dazzling smile brightened Molly's face, but a tiny trace of skepticism showed in her hazel eyes. "Really, Dad? Next year I can camp by myself?"

"Maybe. I'll think about it. Let's see how this year goes first, huh?"

She leaned farther out and wrapped her arms around his neck. "I love you!"

James pulled her the rest of the way out of the window. "I love you, too." After a quick hug, he set her on her feet and took her by the hand. "Now, let's go see about our cabin."

"I'm afraid I assigned your cabin to someone else, dear. Had to separate a pair of volunteer women who don't seem to get along." Trudy Luciano, the camp director, rose from her wooden swivel chair and perched on the front edge of the desk. A rotating fan hummed on the top of an oak filing cabinet, providing some relief from the summer heat. "Don and I figured you'd changed your mind. We both know Jerry pretty much forced you to come."

Rachel toyed with the handle of her bag. "Well, if you've been friends with Jerry for as many years as he says, then you know once he makes up his mind, there's no changing it." Her principal had taken extensive lessons from her father. And when the two men—best friends ever since her father had saved Jerry's life by carrying him on broken ankles from a battlefield after their service chopper had crashed—banded together, people found themselves doing things they really didn't want to. Like getting married. *Or coming here.*

Trudy shook her head and made a sympathetic tsking noise. She had a warm but weathered face and a short, barrel-shaped body. But her orange hair and loud tie-dyed shirt, paired with faded bell-bottom jeans, made the woman resemble Aunt Bee from the old television show time-warped through Woodstock. "Jerry says you're a wonderful teacher, and he's very worried about you."

"Uh-huh."

"Are you sure you want to be here?"

Something in the way she asked made Rachel wonder if the camp director was the one having second thoughts. And frankly, Rachel didn't blame her. Who knew what Jerry had told her? Did he mention the confusion? Well, after showing up on the wrong day, that one ought to be clear. The misplaced plan books? The report cards not finished on time? The thousand little details that slipped her mind of late?

She sighed. "I don't have a choice, Mrs. Luciano."

"Trudy," the woman admonished.

"Trudy. Yes. Right." Rachel shifted in the chair, the bare skin of her thighs unsticking from the wooden surface with an embarrassing sucking noise. "I've been a teacher for ten years, and loved every minute of it. Without my career to keep me occupied this past year, I'm sure I'd have been admitted to the funny farm by now."

She dropped her voice to a whisper and looked down at the faded tile floor. "Since I lost Daniel, it's been my only reason to get out of bed each morning."

"But it's hard to be an effective teacher, dear, if you don't like being around children anymore."

Rachel whipped her head up and met Trudy's frank gaze. "Is that what Jerry said? That's not it at all. I love kids. It's just…"

"It's just what?"

"It's just hard, that's all." Rachel rose from the chair to wander across the office. Sheets of paper with various schedules cluttered a bulletin board. Around the edges, photos of smiling children advertised the joys of summer camp. A little boy with sun-streaked brown hair and sparkling blue eyes caught her attention. How Daniel would have loved camp, the horses and the swimming, the boating…

A heaviness invaded her chest; icy fingers squeezed her heart like the Play-Doh Daniel had loved. Rachel closed her eyes and swallowed hard.

"It's okay to miss him," Trudy said softly from near her shoulder.

Eyes flashing open, Rachel stepped to the side and leaned against the windowsill. She didn't want to discuss it with a strange woman, a woman whose report to Jerry at the end of the session would determine whether Rachel had a career or not. Hell, she didn't want to talk about it with anyone.

But she was going to have to play the game if she wanted to keep teaching second-graders. If the administration, particularly Jerry's boss, the superintendent, didn't think she could handle her job and her grief over losing Daniel, they'd insist she take a medical leave of absence. Which would leave her with nothing to distract her from the pain.

Somehow, Rachel had to convince this woman that she could get close to kids, that she was still a good teacher. "Trudy, is there someplace else I could bunk, since you've reassigned my cabin?"

"You're sure you want to stay?" The woman's green eyes expressed her reservation.

"Yes. I want to stay."

"Good, I'm so glad!" There was genuine

warmth in Trudy's voice. "I've got an empty cabin over in the family loop. The parents here will treat you as a sort of hero—"

"You're not going to tell them?"

Trudy studied her intently for a moment, then shook her head. "I hoped you would."

Rachel tried not to let her dismay show.

The other woman continued, "You're not just here to help us with the kids. You're here because Jerry thinks—and Don and I agree—that seeing the kinds of miracles that can come from tragedy will help you. Don's got a Ph.D. in counseling, and he runs support groups for the parents, and we'd love for you to sit in on some of them."

"I...I don't know if I can. I don't think I want people to know."

"Well, in your own time. Come on, I'll show you where your cabin is."

Rachel let the camp director lead her from the office. She felt numb as she methodically placed one foot in front of the other.

The funny smoke from Trudy's hippie past had apparently addled a few too many of the woman's brain cells. What else would explain the fact that she expected Rachel to tell the parents of transplant children that Daniel, her sweet four-and-a-half-year-old son, her only child, had been an organ donor?

"OH, DAD, ISN'T IT GREAT?" Molly skipped up the steps to the bright blue cabin, the second to last one in the row. A nearly identical structure—this one painted a shade of yellow that reminded James of corn on the cob and melted butter—sat to his right. The dirt road dead-ended in front of it.

He dragged the suitcases from the back of the SUV and followed his daughter. "It's very nice. Wait for me."

He gritted his teeth at the twinge in his right shoulder, compliments of Molly's bag. How many clothes did an eight-year-old need for camp? What else did she have stashed in the case? Books, more than likely. Molly was an avid reader. She'd certainly had plenty of time in her short life to cultivate the hobby. But how many books did it take to make a suitcase over the weight limit for some small bridges?

He looked around. Tall trees—some pine, most hardwood—filled the area across from the cabin. Molly ran her hand across a set of purple metal wind chimes near the front door, setting off a series of melodic tinkling sounds. Several hundred feet behind the cozy wooden structure, a lake beckoned, small ripples slapping gently against the shore.

The peacefulness of the place invited serious relaxation. If he was lucky, maybe there was a hammock nearby. He hadn't had a real vacation since before Molly was born.

"Dad! Come on, hurry up!"

"I'm coming," he muttered, following his

daughter up the steps. The small screened porch contained two folding lawn chairs and a wooden coat tree. James dropped the luggage and searched his pocket for the key.

Molly plastered her nose against the window.

"I can't open it with you in the way, sweet-heart."

She stepped aside to let him unlock the door, then rushed in ahead of him, dodging the table and four chairs near the front windows. James walked past the efficiency kitchen and tossed his carry-on on the blue couch in front of the fireplace.

Molly popped out of a door on the far end of the living room. "I want this bedroom, Dad. I can see the lake from the window!"

James fished a can of disinfectant spray from his bag, returned to the porch to pick up Molly's suit-case and headed into the room she had chosen. Af-ter depositing the hernia-maker on a luggage stand, he began to spray the white wicker furniture.

Molly turned at the hiss of the can. "Dad! Can't you give it a break? Jeez." She threw open the window. "That stuff reeks." The second window in the room resisted, but with a grunt, she shoved it halfway up.

"Germs are—"

"The enemy, yeah, I know."

James nodded. With an immune-suppressed child, he couldn't take germs lightly. The medica-tions that prevented Molly's immune system from attacking her new heart also left her susceptible to sicknesses other kids could brush right off. A summer cold or a virus could turn into something serious, even life-threatening, for Molly. Pins and needles jabbed at the back of his neck, and his shoulder muscles tightened at the thought.

"Stop complaining. Unpack your clothes, then I want you to lie down for a little while." He held up his hand to forestall the whine he saw coming. "Tonight after dinner there's a bonfire to welcome everyone, and you'll probably be up late. So, take your pick. Lie down now for a while, or leave the party early."

She rolled her eyes at him. "Okay, you win."

"That's my girl. I'm going to get the rest of the stuff out of the car."

Molly began unpacking as he headed out. Several large hardcover books appeared from the depths of her bag and James groaned. "Next time, do your old dad a favor and bring paperbacks, would you, tiger?"

She grinned at him, eyes shining. "You're not old, Dad. You're just slightly used."

"Oh, thanks a lot. Was that supposed to be a compliment? If so, you need to work on it a little more."

Slightly used? He pondered the words as he thudded down the cottage steps. Sometimes *badly used* felt more like it. His ex-wife, Tiffany, who rarely contacted their daughter, was responsible for most of that.

And Molly's medical condition had also contributed to the battering he'd taken. All the surgeries she'd needed as the doctors tried to correct her birth defect. All the unknowns. Finally having to put her on the transplant list. And then, the waiting. It was so hard to live your life not knowing if this day would be your child's last. Tiffany hadn't even tried. She'd bolted by the time Molly was five months old and fled to the West Coast.

Sunlight glinted off the polished black surface of a car at the yellow cottage. James blinked, then raised his hand to shield his eyes. It was the GTO convertible belonging to the flustered blond woman. A woman shouldn't be driving it—a classic muscle car—no matter how good she looked in a pair of tight shorts. It was a man's car. Testosterone and leaded fuel.

If the P.C. police knew his thoughts, he'd lose his psychologist license for sure.

But he had to get a closer look at it again. Biting back a grin and the urge to grunt like Tim Allen, he strolled down the dirt lane, one eye on the car, the other on the cabin. When the owner didn't appear, he lost himself in admiration of the machine of his dreams, inspecting it closely from one end to the other.

Bent over the engine some time later, he became aware of the faint scent of lemon and the distinct feeling of warmth behind him. A quick glance over his shoulder confirmed his suspicion. *Busted.*

"Don't you know it's rude to get under someone's hood without permission?"

James straightened, then turned, finding himself close enough to touch the nameless woman.

"Well?" She propped her fists on her hips and eyed him the same way he did Molly when he caught her up to no good.

He forced a casual grin and stole a few seconds of observation time. Her shoulder-length corn-silk hair had been pulled back into a ponytail, and in the bright sunlight, he noticed small lines around her eyes and mouth. Smile lines. Obviously this was a woman with a sense of humor. Only she wasn't smiling now. "Sometimes it's easier to ask forgiveness than it is permission," he said.

One corner of her mouth twitched, then she shook her head. "So you're sorry you're under my hood?"

Could he coax that tiny twitch into a full-blown grin? "I'm sorry if I made you mad. But I'm not sorry I'm under your hood."

Her eyes widened, and she drew a sharp breath. With another shake of her head, she stepped back, clearly delineating the line he'd inadvertently crossed when he'd turned to face her. "Men. You're all the same."

"Aah, so you're harboring some hostility toward my entire gender." As a psychologist who counseled many couples and families, he should know. He often had a ringside seat for the battle between the sexes.

He stole a quick look at her left hand. No wedding ring, but that didn't necessarily mean anything. "This is a great car, and I couldn't resist checking it out." He gestured toward the engine. "Is that a four-hundred-turbo trannie?"

She shrugged. "I don't know."

"You don't know? You own this terrific car, and you don't even know what's under her hood?"

"No, and I don't really care, either. It gets me where I want to go, and that's all that matters."

James closed his mouth to stop it from gaping. After several seconds, he found his voice again. "You want to sell it?"

Her eyes narrowed. She freed the prop stick and slammed the hood, forcing him backward. "It's not for sale. Trust me, you don't have enough money to buy it."

"Try me."

"No. There are some things money can't buy, and this car is one of them."

"A gift from a man friend?" he asked. Though how any man would part with a car like this was beyond him.

Her hollow chuckle lacked humor. "In a manner of speaking. This car belonged to my ex-husband. Now it belongs to me." She ran a palm over the hood, then slapped it soundly.

James winced. Classic displaced aggression. "Not too fond of him, then, are you?"

She looked back up at him. "You know the nickname for this car, James?"

He nodded. "Goat."

"Right. Let's just say I got Roman's goat in the divorce settlement." She folded her arms across her chest, as though daring him to make something of it.

What a tough cookie. Wonder what else she took the poor sucker for? He glanced at the GTO again. "There's no way I'd have let my ex-wife end up with a car like this." No way in hell. She'd gotten enough of his money, but a car like this he'd have fought for.

Just like he would have fought for Molly if he'd had to.

But then, Tiffany hadn't wanted Molly. Couldn't deal with Molly's condition, with the ever-present risk of losing her, with the hospitals and doctors…

The woman's ghost of a smile disappeared, and she lowered her hands to her sides. "I didn't think I'd get it, either. But when a man wants his freedom badly enough, he'll give up just about anything. Including his most prized possession." She kicked the tire. "I didn't ask for anything else. Not alimony, nothing. Just this stupid car." She brushed her sneaker in the loose dirt around the wheel. "A small way to make him pay."

The tough cookie had been replaced by a woman

with obvious wounds. Experience told him there was a lot more to the story than the exchange of a car for freedom. "Ouch. I'm sorry."

Rachel glanced up from the gravel she'd been scuffing with her toe. "Don't be. I'm not. He played, and he paid." Although, there had been a far greater cost to his playing, a cost he'd never be able to compensate for. If he hadn't been so distracted by his new squeeze, maybe Daniel would still be alive.

"So you got his goat, but didn't take him for a ride?"

"Nope. Just wanted his car. You know, hit him where it hurts?"

"Remind me not to mess with you." He smiled broadly at her, showing a solitary dimple deep in his right cheek. Paired with the cleft in his chin, it made him even more attractive. "We never did finish our introduction." He held out his hand. "Since we're going to be neighbors for the next two weeks, maybe we should try again. I'm James McClain."

"Rachel. Rachel Thompson."

"A pleasure to meet you, Rachel." He gave her fingers a light squeeze, then let go. "My daughter, Molly, had a heart transplant a year ago in September. How about you?"

Daughter? Heart transplant? She hadn't seen a child in the back of his car, but then the windows were tinted. She'd gotten the impression he was a single guy without a family, another employee stuck at the far reaches of the family cabin loop due to one of Trudy's assignment mix-ups.

But that wasn't the case. This man had one of those walking miracles she'd been sent here to see. A miracle born of a tragedy like hers.

"Rachel?"

She looked back up into those soft brown eyes, which now shone with concern. "Uh, I—I'm here to observe and teach arts and crafts."

"No kids?"

Damn. Now he'd really done it. Her nose tingled as though someone had poured soda into it, her eyes misted over. She pinched the bridge of her nose hard and struggled for composure. "I have to go. I have lesson plans to write up." She turned on her heel and headed for her cabin. In her mind she could hear her father's clipped voice barking the phrase he'd used so often during her childhood. *"Good little soldiers don't cry."*

Chin cleft and good looks be damned, James McClain was nothing but trouble with his miracle child and probing questions.

CHAPTER TWO

SHE'D SURVIVED A HEART defect and a transplant, but figured she'd eventually die of embarrassment. Caused by her father. He could be such a dork. Molly crossed her eyes and stuck out her tongue at his back as he carried their dinner trays to the garbage cans on the far side of the dining hall.

"I saw that," a soft voice with a faint Southern accent drawled. "What's he done now?"

Molly spun on the bench, then jumped to her feet. "Aah! Cherish!" She flung her arms around her friend and squeezed her tight. "You made it!"

"I told you I was coming." Cherish wiggled from the embrace, then plopped down at the table.

"Yeah, but your biopsy was last week. You were supposed to call me." Molly frowned at the other girl. Rejection right after her transplant a year ago had almost killed Cherish. "How was it?"

"I'm here, aren't I?"

Relief washed through her. "No rejects?"

"Clean as a baby's butt." Cherish grinned and grabbed Molly's hand. "During a bath, that is."

The two girls giggled. "You should know,"

Molly said. "What's it like having a new baby around?"

Cherish wrinkled her nose. "Noisy, stinky and usually wet at both ends." She tugged Molly down onto the seat next to her and whispered in her ear, "But I'll tell you one thing. It sure gives my mom something better to do than fuss over me all the time."

"Jeez, I wish Dad had something better to do."

"You still didn't tell me what he did this time."

Molly swiveled her head to check on her father's return. He was still on the far side of the room, talking to a short lady with orange hair. *Orange? Eewww.* That was even worse than her own red mop.

Molly turned back to her friend. "The usual. Eat this healthy food. Take a nap. Don't overdo it. Wash those hands. Oh, and my very favorite, the disinfectant spray. You know, I could clobber the people who invented disinfectant wipes. Dad wiped down the table and bench when we got here."

"Omigod. How embarrassing. Even my mom's not that bad."

"Tell me about it." Molly searched the dining hall. "Where is your mom? I want to see the baby."

"She's at our cabin, feeding him."

"You came by yourself?"

"Yeah, so? I'm ten, I can come to the dining hall without getting lost."

"Must be nice," Molly muttered.

"Look, your dad will back off a little when you're older."

"Sure. Maybe when I go to high school." Guilt poked at her. Her dad loved her and was only trying to protect and take care of her. He was always there when she needed him. He just hadn't learned to let go when she didn't. If he had his way, she'd still have training wheels on her bike. "Let me ask him if we can go to your cabin."

Molly jumped up, slamming into someone.

"Oh, no! Watch out!" The woman's dinner tray hovered just over Molly's head and she fumbled with it, just barely saving it from crashing to the floor. The contents of a tall plastic glass sloshed over the top and spattered the tray, the woman's meal and her pretty pink shirt.

"I'm sorry!" Molly looked up at the woman's face. Recognition slowly dawned. It was the lady with the sunny blond hair she'd caught Dad staring at earlier.

The woman offered her a slight smile. "No harm done, luckily." Her smile wavered. "You nearly wore my dinner."

"I...I should have looked where I was going."

"Like I said, no harm done. Have a nice night." The lady circled around her and scanned the room, finally choosing a seat at an empty table in the far corner.

Something better to do, huh? Molly thought

about what she'd told Cherish. Maybe a new lady friend would keep her dad busy so Molly could enjoy her time at camp without being smothered. Besides, he needed someone in his life. They both needed someone.

She'd overheard conversations between Dad and Gram, and knew her mother had been a big disappointment to him—Gram's words, not his—but maybe in a place like this Molly could find a woman who didn't think kids with new hearts were such a big deal. Maybe the blond lady? She didn't have any kids with her.

"Uh-oh, what are you thinking?" Cherish asked. "I know that look. It's the I-have-a-plan-that's-going-to-get-us-into-trouble look."

Molly grinned. "Yep, I have a plan. And you're going to help me. I think Dad needs something better to do at camp than worry about me, and I think maybe a girlfriend is just what he needs."

The two girls burst into giggles, then hooked their pinkies together. "Best friends for life?" Cherish asked.

"Best friends for life," Molly agreed. "And then some."

RACHEL EASED FARTHER INTO the shadows, resting her back against a gnarled tree. A roaring bonfire and lit torches illuminated the man-made beach along the lake. The chatter of families mingled with pops and crackles as the fire shifted; the aroma of burning wood filled the air.

"Hi, again." The little girl from the dining hall held out a thin stick with something on the end. "I brought you a toasted marshmallow to say I'm sorry for running into you."

"That was very thoughtful." Rachel pushed off the tree and bent over, trying to get a good peek in the dim light. "Are you sure you don't want it yourself?"

The child lifted one shoulder. "I've had my limit. I made this one for you."

"Thank you." Rachel's fingers sank into the gooey peace offering, and she tugged it off the end of the stick, then popped it into her mouth. "Mmm, delicious." Actually, it was a burnt cinder surrounding molten goo, but she didn't want to hurt the child's feelings. She swallowed and forced a smile. "I haven't had a toasted marshmallow in a long time. Thanks again."

"You're welcome." The little girl grinned. "Where are your kids?"

Rachel coughed and shook her head.

"You don't have any?"

Someday, maybe she'd figure out the right way to answer this question, a way that acknowledged Daniel but didn't reveal the depth of her pain. For now, she took the easy way. "No."

"Don't you like kids?"

"I'm a teacher." As if that guaranteed liking kids.

The corners of the child's mouth spread further. "Cool. Are you married?"

"No, I'm not." She had to get this conversation back into safer territory. "Are you?"

The little girl giggled. "Not yet." She rolled her eyes heavenward. "Probably never if my dad has his way. Speaking of Dad—" she whipped her head around, pigtails flying "—I gotta go. Later." She scampered off into the crowd surrounding the bonfire.

Cute kid. I wonder which of her siblings had a transplant? Rachel worked a cinder loose from a molar with her tongue and discreetly got rid of it. Why kids thought marshmallows had to go up in flames to be toasted was beyond her. But still, it had been a sweet gesture.

It reminded her of the time Daniel decided to make breakfast for her. Captain Crunch cereal, orange juice and toast. That toast had launched her into laughter for weeks—outside of Daniel's hearing, of course. Burned to the point of being something she could have used as a roof tile, the toast had peanut butter, jelly, honey and cream cheese piled on top of it—her son's effort to "cover up the black part." And she'd eaten every bite with a smile and done her best to keep it down. Kids…

The familiar ache began to build inside her chest, and she did her best to keep that down, too.

A blast of feedback from a sound system shrieked, then someone blew into a microphone, intoning the standard ''Testing, one, two,'' followed by the mandatory taps on the head of the mike. ''Is this thing working?''

''Yes!'' Several voices answered at once.

''Good, good,'' the man continued. ''Just in case I didn't get to greet you today, I'm Donald Luciano. I run this camp with my wife, Trudy.'' The crowd broke into applause, and he held up a hand. ''Now, now, you might want to wait until the end of camp to see if you still feel like applauding me.''

''We love ya, Don!'' someone yelled.

''Camp Firefly Wishes is the best!'' added another youthful voice.

Don chuckled and ran a hand over his scraggly beard. ''We like to think so. I want to welcome you all to camp, and officially open the session with the traditional lighting of the memory torch.''

A low hum passed through the crowd. People shuffled their feet in the sand. The hair on the back of Rachel's neck rose. *Memory torch?*

Trudy joined her husband on the sand near the small sound system. Painted stripes in the spectrum of the rainbow swirled down the handle of the white torch she carried.

Don cleared his throat. ''Those of you who've been here before know this is our way of remembering those we've lost. Most of us know people who never made it off the transplant lists, people who died waiting.''

Trudy moved closer and laid a hand on her husband's shoulder. The pair exchanged a glance so filled with support and a special bond that Rachel felt a sharp pang of envy. Loving support from a spouse would be most welcome at this moment.

Don reached up and patted his wife's hand before continuing. ''Our adult son was one of them. That's why we opened this camp. But this torch will burn brightly all while camp is in session, to remind us. We also want to dedicate it to the memory of those whose death gave others a second chance at life. This is for the donors and their families.''

Rachel stumbled backward until she bumped into the tree. She reached out and gripped the bark tightly between her fingers. As Trudy passed the torch to her husband and he lowered it to the flames of the bonfire, Rachel closed her eyes.

She inhaled the cool night air deeply, then exhaled slowly. Without thinking, she pinched the bridge of her nose between her thumb and index finger to make the tingles go away—a habit she'd developed since Daniel's death.

''Whatever you're keeping locked inside you will eat you alive if you don't let it out.'' The deep, yet soft voice came from her side.

Rachel opened her eyes and lowered her hand. ''James.'' She crammed all thoughts of Daniel into the small compartment of her heart where she tried to keep him. "Not only do you get under my hood, but you want to get inside my head, too, hmm?"

He lifted one shoulder, cocking his head to the side. "Can't help it."

"And why is that?"

"I'm a psychologist. Comes naturally to me."

Oh, great. Just what she needed, a hunky psychologist with a miracle kid who wanted to crawl inside her mind and psyche. Granted, the rest of her didn't seem to appeal to men. Her ex-husband, the snake, the charmer, had always said he'd been attracted to her intelligence. But then he'd left her for a woman whose boobs were larger than her IQ.

Of course, the marriage had been built on very shaky ground to start with.

You are not interested in another man. Men are nothing but trouble. And this one has a child, a sick little girl who had a heart transplant. Think how much potential for pain there is in that. Haven't you had enough?

"Rachel? Are you all right?"

Her fingernails sank into the tree trunk again. "I'm fine. Thanks for asking." He stood so close she could smell his after-shave, a rugged, masculine musk that went well with his chiseled facial features, blue jeans and shirt patterned in a Native American motif. "You don't look like a psychologist."

He smiled. "And just what is a psychologist supposed to look like?"

"Well, there are two schools of thought on that. One is the stuffy, suit-wearing, tie-and-glasses psychologist who ran rats through mazes in college and now sits behind his desk with a clipboard, murmuring 'Ah-ha' and 'I see.' They like to run IQ tests and personality profiles."

"And the other?"

"The New Age, bearded, potbellied psychologist who burns incense. Kinda looks like Don over there. In college, instead of running rats through a maze, he set them free. He says things like 'And how does that make you feel?' and 'What do *you* think about it?'"

"And you base these stereotypes on…?"

"I work with a few of the first type at school."

"What about the second ones?"

"I've run into a few of them, here and there." And none of the therapists she'd seen—at other people's urging—had helped. None of them understood that she just wasn't ready.

"Marriage counseling?" He stared intently at her mouth. "You mentioned your ex earlier."

"Sort of."

Music swelled in the background. Peering around his shoulder, Rachel could see Don and several other campers with guitars, gearing up for a sing-along. Camp songs about poison ivy and missing meatballs and green speckled frogs, she could handle, but if they got sappy, she would simply leave.

She turned back to James and caught him still

staring at her. "What? Why are you looking at me like that?"

"You've got something stuck on the corner of your mouth." He cupped her chin with one hand and ran the pad of his other thumb over the crease in her lips. "Whatever it is, it's sticky."

His hands were warm, touching her lightly yet confidently, conveying quiet strength. Her muscles softened like the inside of that marshmallow…. She chuckled, more from nerves at his touch than humor. "That's my burnt offering."

"Burnt offering?" He made another pass with his finger over her lips. "I can't get it. It's going to need something more. Sorry." The hand cupping her chin vanished.

She ran her tongue along the juncture of her lips several times, then used a fingernail to scrape at it. "Did I get it?"

"Uh, yeah, you got it."

"Thanks. Wouldn't want to walk around with marshmallow on my face all night."

"Daddy?"

James stiffened at Molly's voice behind him. He backed away from Rachel and whirled to face his daughter. "Yeah, tiger?"

"I just wondered where you were, that's all."

His cheeks grew warm, and guilt spread over him like refrigerated honey. "I'm sorry, Molly. I thought you were with Cherish and her family?"

"I was, but they're going back to their cabin. The

baby's getting fussy, and her mom says she's not feeding him in a crowd of people.'' Molly craned her neck to peek around him. ''Who are you talking to?''

''Just…our neighbor.'' James stepped aside. ''Molly, this is Rachel. Rachel, this is my daughter, Molly.''

Rachel gaped. ''This…this is your daughter?''

''Yes.''

''We've kinda met, Dad. I bumped into her at dinner.''

James looked from Rachel to his daughter. ''Bumped into her? Literally?''

''Um, yes.'' Molly batted her lashes at him and grinned. ''No biggie, though. Right?''

James swung his gaze back from child to woman. ''No biggie?''

Rachel shook her head. ''No biggie. She apologized.'' She edged away from the tree and around them. ''I have to get back to my cabin. Busy day tomorrow.''

He reached out and brushed his hand against her elbow. ''What's the rush? We'll walk back with you.''

Rachel leaned in closer to him, pitched her voice low. ''I thought you said your daughter had a heart transplant?''

''I did,'' Molly piped up, obviously picking up the words not intended for her. ''Wanna see my scar?''

"No!" Rachel's eyes widened; the moonlight illuminated a wildness in them. "No, I don't—" She stumbled sideways, and when James reached to steady her, she extended her palm to ward him off. "I...really have to go now."

With that, she took off.

"Oops. Sorry, Dad." His daughter's small hand slipped into his own, and she gave it a squeeze.

He leaned over and planted a kiss on the top of her head. "It's all right, Unsinkable. Some people just don't do well with things like that." *Like your mother.* And obviously his new neighbor. He tempered an unexpected surge of disappointment at the thought. "I've warned you before about flashing that scar. I'm glad it doesn't bother you, but you have to be considerate about other people's feelings. Besides, a little modesty would be a good thing."

"You take your shirt off outside."

"I'm not a girl," he whispered into her ear. "You can't do that."

"Why not, for now? It's not like I have b—"

"Molly!" He glared at his daughter. "This discussion is over. Let's go. It's time for bed, anyway."

JAMES TUCKED THE FLORAL bedspread around Molly's sides, then sat down, causing the wicker frame to creak. "Only ten minutes for reading tonight. It's late already, and tomorrow you have a lot of stuff going on.''

"Okay, Dad.'' Molly picked at a piece of lint on the covers. "Do you think that lady hates me now?''

"No, of course not. I think you caught her by surprise, is all.'' Rachel's reaction, however, had been a surprise to him. That made twice she'd bolted when confronted with his daughter's condition.

"Good.'' Molly sighed. "Do you think she's pretty? I think she is. I wish I had hair like that instead of this stupid red crud.''

"Your hair isn't really red, it's auburn. With a few flaming highlights.'' He ran his hand over her soft waves. "I wouldn't want it any other way. Someday, Unsinkable, you're going to be a real heartbreaker, and I'm going to have to keep the boys at bay with a very large bat.''

"Sure. With all these freckles. And I don't want to be a heartbreaker. Mommy broke your heart, and it hasn't been fixed. I hate her. Too bad Dr. Nelinski couldn't give you a new heart, too.''

James shifted back at the animosity in her voice. "Hey now, where is all this coming from?''

Molly's mouth curved downward and she avoided his eyes. "Nowhere.''

"It's coming from somewhere. It's okay to talk about it. You're entitled to your feelings.''

"It's...never mind. How come you don't go out on dates like other divorced parents?"

"Whoa. How old are you now? Seventeen? I don't think my dating is really your business, tiger."

"But why don't you? Cherish's mom found Nolan, and now they're a real family."

"Aah, I see." James leaned over and tapped gently on her nose. "I don't date, sweetheart, because you are a very special girl, and I would have to find a very, very special lady to be good enough for us. Second chances aren't easy to come by."

"But I got a second-chance heart."

James let his palm rest at the base of her throat. Overwhelming love rushed through him with every steady thump beneath his hand. "Yes," he whispered. "Thank God, you did. And that's the only second chance I need." He brushed his lips over her forehead, ever vigilant of the temperature of her skin. "I love you, Unsinkable."

She groaned. "I love you, too, but I hate that name."

"I know. It's a father's privilege to give his daughter a nickname she can't stand. Lights out in ten." The bed creaked again. He headed for his own room.

The half-drawn shade slapped against the window, thanks to the cool night breeze. When he flipped the wall switch, the lightbulb flashed and popped. With a mumbled curse, James cautiously headed for the bedside table, hoping for better luck with the lamp there. He stopped short as he passed the window.

A soft yellow glow illuminated the neighboring cabin. "Rachel Thompson," he murmured. "What's your story?" His thoughts wandered to the flicker of pain he'd seen in her eyes at their first meeting. There was obviously more to Rachel than she was prepared to reveal. Then the image of her walking away from him flashed into his consciousness. "Stop that," he muttered as the light next door flicked off. He didn't need a flesh-and-blood woman tempting him. This trip was for Molly. Her needs came first, as always. His needs...well, his needs could wait. They'd waited this long.

CHAPTER THREE

"I'M STUCK!"

The panicked cry from the far side of the arts-and-crafts room reached Rachel, and she jerked her head up, dropping the pipe-cleaner antenna she was helping Sean glue to his bell bug project.

"Miss Rachel!" Molly waved at her from a table near the windows. "Help! My friend is stuck!"

"Stuck?" She crossed the room in several quick strides. Great. First full day on the job and something had already gone wrong. Well, that was a Monday for you. "What do you mean, she's stuck?" The only glue they were using was white glue, and that wasn't likely to get children stuck. At least, not in her experience.

"Ow! Molly, don't!"

Rachel glanced down. The child's arm, trapped just above her elbow, protruded between the slats in the back of the old wooden school chair. "How did you manage that?"

"I don't know, but I can't get it out!" The girl sniffed and tugged on her arm to demonstrate. "Ow!"

"Let's see what we can do here." Rachel

grasped the child's shoulder. "What's your name again, sweetie?" She pushed backward.

"Cherish! Ouch, stop!"

"Well, Cherish, you certainly do good work."

The rest of the eight-to-ten-year-old group gathered around, chattering to one another. "Hey, maybe they'll have to cut your arm off," one of the boys suggested.

Cherish's face lightened two shades.

"No one is going to cut your arm off." Rachel glared at the boy. "Cut the chair, maybe, but not you."

"Please, get me out! It really hurts!" The girl started to inhale and exhale quickly.

"I once heard this story about this guy who caught his leg in a bear trap, and to get out, he cut his leg off, only he cut off the wrong one and—"

Cherish moaned and Rachel whirled on the other children. "That is quite enough! All of you get back to your seats, now!"

The kids scrambled to obey.

Rachel tried once more to pull the little girl free.

Cherish gasped and grabbed her chest. "Oh, I hate this!"

The blood rushed from Rachel's skull, and she went light-headed. She turned to Molly, who'd remained at her friend's side, stroking Cherish's shoulder. "Is she like you? A transplant kid?"

Molly nodded. "Cherish got her heart a few months before me."

Panic clouded Rachel's brain and she struggled to process the fact that she had a trapped child, a child with a heart condition, clutching at her chest. "Molly, get me the container of soap from the sink." She looked over her shoulder without waiting to see if Molly complied. "Sean, you run, and I mean run, to the medical office and get the doctor. Move!" The boy dashed for the doorway.

Rachel knelt and stroked Cherish's trapped arm. "You need to calm down. I'm going to get you out of here. Everything's going to be fine." *Please, let it be fine!*

"Here's the soap." Molly thrust the container at her. "What are you going to do?"

"I'm going to get your friend out of this chair." Rachel pumped the thick liquid on Cherish's arm, both above the chair slats and below, then carefully spread it. "How are you doing, sweetie?"

The child opened her eyes to stare down at her. "Okay. You think that will really work?"

"Of course it will. No problem." Rachel added a few more squirts for good measure.

"What is the trouble, ladies?" Dr. Santebe asked in a singsong accent as he crossed the room. A reassuring smile flashed gleaming white teeth against his olive complexion. He shoved aside the art projects on the table and perched his hip on the edge, leaning down to brush a finger over Cherish's cheek.

"I think I can get her arm out, but she seems to have a pain in her chest," Rachel said.

"This is so?" he asked the girl.

Cherish shrugged her shoulders, then winced. "Ow. Yeah, but my heart was just catching up, that's all. I panicked."

"Thank you, Dr. Cherish. Might I take a listen?" The physician pulled his stethoscope from around his neck and placed the pieces in his ears as Cherish nodded permission.

While the child was distracted, Rachel gently grasped the trapped arm in one hand and the bony shoulder in her other. She gave a quick, hard shove, and Cherish slipped free from the chair.

"Yes!" Molly shouted. "You did it!"

Rachel looked at the doctor, who nodded at her while removing his stethoscope. "She is fine. Good work." He took Cherish's hand and examined the angry red blotch where her arm had been pinned. "I think we will put some ice on this after we rinse the soap. Come, we will go to my office."

Rachel climbed unsteadily to her feet as the doctor assisted the girl from the chair. "What happened with her chest?"

"In a transplant, the organ nerves are severed. So when a heart transplant patient becomes excited, or exercises, the heart does not know to speed up. Sometimes a pounding sensation occurs in the chest when it does so suddenly."

"So, she's okay?"

A buzzer rang, announcing lunchtime, and the kids scrambled from their chairs to swarm toward the door where some parents already awaited them. "Hey, make sure everything is cleaned up before you go!" Rachel shouted over the pandemonium before looking back to the doctor.

"She is fine." The doctor gripped Rachel's hand and smiled at her. "Good idea with the soap. I will remember this. Come, Cherish, let us find your parents and get some ice for your arm."

Molly followed them as far as the back of the room, where she began to help clean up.

Rachel sank onto the edge of the table and covered her face with trembling fingers, the adrenaline rush fading as her pulse throbbed in her skull. She inhaled deeply and slowly exhaled, trying to compose herself.

"A little excitement, huh?"

Rachel lowered her hands to find James standing nearby. "Just a tad." In the back, Molly and several other children placed finished projects on the drying tables and tidied up the work areas with the help of some other parents. "How do you do it?"

"Do what?"

"Live with the fear that you could lose her at any time?"

His eyebrows tightened and drew downward, and a scowl twisted his mouth. "First of all, don't you ever, ever say anything like that within earshot of my daughter." He glanced over his shoulder, then turned back to her. "Second, don't shoot your mouth off when you have no clue what you're talking about."

"I'm…I'm sorry, I just—"

"No excuses. Positive thinking, positive speaking, positive outcome. So please don't talk negatively around my kid." He turned and walked away.

"But I do have a clue about that fear," she whispered. At least, now she had a clue. When she'd been a parent, she'd been oblivious to that kind of fear. Despite being concerned and safety-minded, she'd never lived with the constant threat of losing her child. But now she knew all too well how quickly life could change.

THE CROWDED LUNCHROOM hummed with the happy chatter of kids and parents along with the clink of utensils against dishes. Somewhere a baby wailed. Rachel lingered in the doorway, debating going in. Her stomach hadn't settled since the excitement of Cherish's ordeal, and the smell of grilled chicken and burgers did little to help.

"Miss Rachel, Miss Rachel!" A redheaded blur streaked in her direction from the other side of the room, arms waving madly.

She glanced toward the door, contemplating a quick exit, when she noticed another orange head gazing in her direction. Trudy Luciano was on the job, eagle eyes trained directly on her from beneath a rainbow sweatband.

"Oof." Rachel exhaled sharply as Molly collided with her. The little girl wrapped her arms around Rachel's middle and squeezed tightly.

"Thank you! You were so great!"

Rachel stiffened, muscles contracting. Trudy was still watching. Rachel patted Molly on the back several times. Not only was a hug from a child something she'd become uncomfortable with, but this one's father was still annoyed with her, judging by the scowl he sent her from a table in the far corner.

And now Trudy was moving in her direction.

Aah, summer camp. Toss in a case of poison ivy and some stinging insects, and life didn't get much better than this.

Your job depends on this, she reminded herself. Jerry had been covering for her with the superintendent for a while now, and this was her last chance to make a good impression. She had to get a favorable report from the camp directors, had to prove she could get her act together.

"Come and eat with us, Miss Rachel," Molly invited, looking up at her. "There's room at our table. Cherish is back from the doctor's office and you can meet her parents."

"Thank you, Molly, but I don't—"

Trudy brushed past. "I heard all about your quick thinking earlier. Good job. And I think having lunch with this child is a wonderful idea." The woman pushed the sweatband higher on her fore-head, the multicolors clashing with her mane of hair. "Perhaps Camp Firefly Wishes is already working its magic on you?"

Rachel forced a smile and disentangled herself from Molly's embrace. "Perhaps it is." She gave Molly's ponytail a gentle tug. "I'll join you in a minute." The girl's quick grin showed a missing side tooth, then she turned and skipped off, back toward her father.

Trudy shook her head and tutted. "It's sad, isn't it?"

"What?"

"A sweet little girl like that with no mama." The woman's green eyes followed the child's progress back to her table. "And with such a handsome daddy." She looked at Rachel.

"He's…easy enough on the eyes."

Trudy's face lit up, and she patted Rachel's shoulder before moving off.

Several minutes later, tray laden with a salad, bread and butter, and iced tea, Rachel approached the table, hoping no one would notice the trembling that made the tea in the glass rock from side to side.

The only empty spot was next to James. A petite brunette woman rocked a fussing baby in her arms while the lanky blond-haired man on the other side of James stretched across the table, trying to pop a pacifier into the tiny mouth.

"I hope—Molly invited me to join you."

James glanced up. The apprehension in Rachel's blue eyes softened the tightness in his chest. Which irritated him all the more. He ground his teeth together, wanting to hold on to his anger with both hands to offset the temptation of wanting to hold on to *her*. When he'd seen her shaking after Cherish's mishap, gathering her into his arms had been an overwhelming impulse. Until she'd made her little comment about the possibility of losing Molly at any time. He reminded himself of how his ex used to say the same thing.

Her tray rattled ominously as he continued to stare at her. Finally, he shifted along the bench. No sense in making a scene in front of everyone. "Have a seat."

Molly and Cherish giggled and bent their heads together to whisper. Molly jumped to her feet. "We're going to get some dessert. We'll be back."

"Fruit, young lady," he reminded. "No sweets. You ate enough marshmallows last night to equal that giant marshmallow guy in the *Ghostbusters* movie."

Molly rolled her eyes at him. "Funny, Dad. Very funny. *Not*."

The rest of the adults chuckled as the girls trotted off.

The man on the other side of James cleared his throat and raised his voice as the baby broke into lung-stretching screams. "Aren't you going to introduce us, James?'' He jerked his head in Rachel's direction.

"Yeah, sorry. Rachel Thompson, this is Nolan and Michelle Driscoll, Cherish's parents.''

"It's a pleasure to meet you. That was good thinking, using soap to get Cherish out of that chair. Thank you.'' Michelle struggled to her feet. "I'm sorry, but I've got to feed Tyler before he breaks everyone's eardrums.''

"I'll come with you, honey. I'm sure James will spare one eye for Cherish.'' Nolan leapt from the bench, pausing to lean over and whisper in James's ear, "Make sure Cherish gets to her next activity, will you, Jimbo? This kid is due for a nap after his feeding, and then it's a little R and R for Mommy and Daddy.''

Nolan straightened up and waggled his eyebrows, then winked at James before escorting his wife from the room.

"I guess I sure know how to clear a table, don't I?'' Rachel murmured.

"Looks that way.''

The blue eyes widened. She picked up her tray and rose to her feet. "This was a mistake. I'll find someplace else to sit.''

"Just sit down and eat. You're already here, and there's not much lunch period left.'' He took her tray and set it back on the table. "Not that there's much here for you to eat. No wonder you're so damn thin.''

"You have a degree in nutrition as well?"

"I've become something of an expert in healthy diets."

"Because of Molly?"

"No, because my eighty-two-year-old grandmother is in training for the Ironman Competition."

Rachel paused in the middle of lifting a forkful of salad to her mouth and shook her head. "You're awfully sarcastic for a psychologist. Or is it just me that brings out the worst in you?"

"It's just you."

She set the fork back down. "Look, James, I'm really sorry I upset you earlier. I certainly had no intention of doing so. I was coming down from a state of panic over Cherish, and I—"

"Said the first thing that came to mind." He sighed.

The niggling image of her leaning against the tree last night, eyes shut, breathing ragged, reminded him that this was a woman who was covering up some kind of pain. He didn't own the market on pain, and he shouldn't be acting like such a damn jackass. After all, she hadn't knowingly parroted Tiffany's words to him. He cleared his throat. "I overreacted. It's just that I don't like Molly to hear any negative thoughts. Things are tough enough for her, I don't like to make matters worse."

"She doesn't seem like her health is uncertain. In fact, I have to confess, I can't tell the transplant kids from the siblings around here.'' Rachel returned to eating.

''That's a wonderful thing to say to the parent of a transplant kid. Because if you could have seen most of them before their transplants, you'd never believe these are the same kids.''

''Did Molly look different? If you don't mind me asking?''

''Yeah, she did. Very much.'' He chugged the last few swallows of his pop to avoid saying anything else. A mental picture of his little girl, pale and too tired to play, taunted him.

''Was she always sick? I mean, what makes a child need a new heart?''

''In her case, a congenital defect. She had a lot of corrective surgeries, but in the end, transplant was the only option.''

Rachel's face lost its color and she dropped her gaze to her plate. She pushed a cherry tomato around her salad bowl with her fork.

''Rachel?''

She briefly met his gaze, then quickly looked down at her tray, but not before he'd seen a shimmering in her eyes.

He reached out and gently clasped her hand. ''What is it? Sharing sometimes eases the burden. And I can assure you, I've pretty much heard it all in my practice.''

''Dad! Dad, guess what?'' Molly and Cherish skidded to a stop next to the table.

James yanked his hand back from Rachel's.

"Where did Mom and Nolan go? Oh, man, I can't believe this," Cherish wailed.

"Why, what's wrong?" Rachel asked.

"I signed them up for the adults' three-legged-race, and now they're not here. There'll be prizes and everything!"

"I'm sure they'll be disappointed," Rachel said, hiding a small smile behind her buttered roll.

"Yes, very," James agreed solemnly. Although he was fairly certain Nolan had a different sort of sporting event in mind for him and his wife.

A brief pang of envy rolled over him.

"But that's okay," Molly announced, "because we've got more news."

"You do?" James eyed his daughter warily. "What?"

"I signed you up for the race, too."

"Molly! Who am I supposed to race with?"

The hazel eyes lit with glee. "With Miss Rachel, of course."

"THIS IS SILLY," JAMES muttered as he tied their ankles together with a rag provided by the enthusiastic Trudy. He picked up another scrap of fabric and moved to their knees, trying to keep his hands and mind from registering how soft her skin was and just how much of that skin was pressing against his.

"Mmm," Rachel hummed, in what he took to

be her agreement. "But your little girl looked so excited about the idea. Besides, it's been a long time since I did anything…fun."

James glanced up in time to catch the fleeting expression of sorrow in her eyes. "And why is that?" he asked gently.

"Guess I just haven't been in a very fun mood lately."

"For any particular reason?"

She leaned over and tugged at the binding around their knees, effectively letting him know she didn't want to talk about it—whatever *it* was. Her divorce, maybe? He knew well enough how that experience could sour someone on fun for a long time.

"Too tight?" He loosened the strip of cloth. "How's that?"

When she approved, he knotted the binding. "Good. Then let's practice, shall we?" He hooked his right arm around her waist. "Bend your outside leg and push off."

After a few false starts, they managed to make their way to the starting line. Molly and Cherish waved at them from the sidelines, and James waved back.

At the far end of the field, Trudy Luciano and another counselor held a yellow tape across the finish line. Don raised a megaphone to his mouth. "Okay, racers! When you hear the tone, you can start. There will be a special prize for the winners of the race. On your mark, get set…'' The mega-phone hooted and the race was on.

"Outside leg first!" James reminded her.

Outside, inside, outside, inside. Rachel chanted to herself as they stumbled down the field. The wind tossed her hair into her face, obscuring her vision.

"Go, Dad, go! You can do it!"

The excitement and confidence in his daughter's voice, a reminder of a child's unwavering faith in a parent, touched something deep within Rachel. "Come on, James, faster!"

He tightened his grip on her, practically lifting her off the field. They charged onward.

They pounded across the finish line, yellow tape streaming around them. Rachel's foot hit a rock and she staggered. The two of them tumbled in a heap, face first into the grass.

She turned her head to the left and found him grinning at her. A chuckle burst from deep within her. "Not exactly a graceful finish, but we did it!"

"That we did."

"Dad! Are you hurt?" Molly rushed to James's side.

"No, tiger, we're fine. We just have to figure out how to get back on our feet from this dignified po-sition."

A booming, masculine laugh echoed over them. "I can help with that. Just hold still while I cut you loose."

Rachel felt tugging against her leg as Don used a pocketknife to cut the ties that bound them together.

Once free, they both rolled over in opposite directions. James offered his hand, then pulled her up.

Cherish and Molly, along with a bunch of children from Rachel's morning's arts-and-crafts program, jumped up and down around them, screaming congratulations.

"Well done!" Don clapped James on the shoulder. He lifted the megaphone into the air and pressed the alarm.

"Folks, I'd like to announce that our winners, James and Rachel, have just won themselves a romantic dinner for two at the nearby Giordano's Italian restaurant!"

Applause from the crowd didn't come close to matching the thundering in Rachel's head. *A romantic dinner for two?* "But we're not a couple, we were just racing together...."

"Way cool, Dad," Molly said. "A date!" She gave Cherish a high five and the pair giggled and hugged each other.

A date?

James went very still beside her. His eyes held the same flicker of mixed apprehension and horror she'd seen in small boys headed for the principal's office.

She understood how he felt.

This was not good. Not good at all.

CHAPTER FOUR

"THIS IS GREAT," MOLLY whispered to Cherish on Tuesday morning during arts and crafts.

"I dunno, Mol. Neither one of them looked real happy when they found out yesterday. And did you notice that Miss Rachel kinda disappeared after that?" Cherish reached across Molly and grabbed the glue bottle.

"She did not. She had to do arts and crafts with the little kids in the afternoon."

"I didn't see her at dinner or the night activities, did you?"

"No," Molly admitted, working a yarn mane onto her lion puppet. "So how else are we gonna get my dad to notice her?"

"Getting him to actually take her for that dinner would be good."

"I'll try."

"Tell him she'll be disappointed if he doesn't. Nolan hates it when Mom is disappointed in him." Cherish pushed back her hair, tucking it behind her ear. A tiny pink gemstone sparkled in her earlobe.

Molly sighed. "Tell me again how you managed to convince your mom to let you pierce your ears."

Cherish grinned. "I made Mom promise that if my biopsy was okay, she'd ask Dr. Nelinski. He said as long as I was really, really careful about keeping them clean to prevent infection, then it would be okay."

Molly propped her chin in her palm. "One more thing Dad will never let happen." Several tables over, Miss Rachel was helping another girl cut out a trunk for an elephant. "Do you think he even likes her a little?" she whispered. If her father didn't like Miss Rachel at all, then Molly would have to find another lady to distract him. But there weren't too many women around without husbands. Besides, she'd already taken a liking to Miss Rachel.

Cherish laughed. "Didn't you see the way he was looking at her yesterday, just before the race? He likes her, all right."

"Shh! Here she comes." Molly smiled as Miss Rachel approached their table.

"How's it going, girls? I trust no one is getting stuck today?"

"Nope," Molly responded. "Will you have lunch with us again?"

"Oh, I don't know. I have to—"

"Miss Rachel! Your purse is ringing!" Sean yelled.

Rachel glanced over her shoulder. "Thank you." She smiled tentatively at James's daughter. "I'll have to get back to you."

Saved by the bell.

She wasn't nearly as happy about the call several minutes later, after listening to her principal's nervous small talk. "Okay, Jer. Now, why'd you really call?" She scanned the art room for hot spots, then wagged a finger. "Jamie, get those scissors away from your hair and back on the project where they belong. You're way too old for that kind of nonsense. This is not beauty school."

"Sounds like you're busy, Rachel. I'll call back later."

"Oh, no you don't. If you were looking for a report on how I'm doing, you would have called your friend Trudy. Out with it."

"I had a meeting with the superintendent this morning. He was very interested in how you're doing at the camp. Wanted to know if you were making progress, dealing with your—" Jerry cleared his throat "—uh, emotional issues, as he called them."

Rachel left the art room, leaning against the wall just outside the door for support. Emotional issues! Her son had died, and the superintendent was talking about "emotional issues." Hell yeah, it was an emotional issue! "And you told him?"

"I told him you were working on it, Rachel." Jerry's voice softened. "How *is* it going, champ?"

"It's going…great, Jer." How did he think it was going? She was surrounded by kids whose lives had been saved by transplants. Kids who'd survived. While hers…hadn't.

"Don't pull that with me. I'm just worried about you, that's all."

Rachel pinched the bridge of her nose. She peered at her students through the square window in the door, making sure they were doing what they should be, that no one was trapped in a chair or cutting their hair. "I know, Jerry. And I appreciate it. I just don't know that you can order this kind of healing, although I know my dad likes to think he can."

He chuckled gruffly. "If anybody could order it, it would be the Sarge. But he's as concerned about you as I am, don't mistake it."

"I know."

"In fact, lots of people are concerned about you. Roman called me this morning."

The muscles along her neck knotted, and she growled into the phone. "What's the rule about mentioning that man's name?" She didn't care if Roman was Jerry's only nephew, he knew where she stood on hearing about him.

"Not to. But, Rachel—"

"Don't you 'but Rachel' me. You send me to this camp, call me up to tell me the superintendent is still concerned about my fitness in the classroom, and then you throw Roman at me? What's next?"

A long sigh floated from the phone receiver. "I hate being caught between the two of you. You know I love you as if you were my own daughter, but Roman *is* my blood. I hate the hurt he's put you through, but I can't turn my back on him any more than I can you, though your father would sure be happy if I washed my hands of Roman."

"I'm not asking you to. Just don't talk to me about him. And don't talk to him about me. He's out of my life now, and that's that." There wasn't anything left to connect them, not even their child. Though they'd been separated for several months before the accident, she'd only taken back her maiden name when the divorce became final. She wanted no link to the man she held responsible for her baby's death.

She shook the phone, then blew across the mouthpiece. "I think my battery's going dead, Jer. I'll call you later in the week." Flipping the phone closed, she returned to the room, the chatter of the kids washing over her. The scents of glue and paper, of drying wildflowers picked by the group of five-to-seven-year-olds the previous afternoon, stirred feelings of loss and longing within her.

If she wasn't a mother anymore, and the superintendent removed her from the classroom so that she was no longer a teacher, then what was she?

Nothing.

"JAMES, I'M GLAD YOU COULD join the group today." Don stuck out his hand. "But I hope you left your psychologist's hat in your cabin. Today you're a transplant parent, like the rest of the folks."

James shifted the lawn chair to his left hand and

clasped Don's right hand with his own. "I'll try, but you know, it's not easy to take that hat off."

Don chortled. "Tell me about it. There are times when Trudy gets so damn mad at me. 'Stop counseling me and argue!'" he mimicked with a smile.

Other parents were unfolding the chairs, arranging them in a circle in the shade of the gently swaying oaks. Nolan trudged across the lawn, chairs in either hand. Michelle followed with Tyler in a front-carrier. She waved to James, and he returned the gesture.

"Well, would you look at that. I didn't think she'd do it," Don murmured.

James followed his glance. Rachel stood off to the side of the group, biting her lower lip and scanning the crowd. Her rigid posture spoke volumes on the subject of her discomfort. James had taken a step in her direction before he'd even realized it, only to be stopped by Don's hand on his arm.

"Don't. Do me a favor, don't sit anywhere near her. The impression I've gotten of her is she's not going to open up if anyone gets too close. And believe me, that young woman needs to open up."

"I know that. In fact, I practically told her so the first night of camp."

"You did? And how did she respond?"

"She ignored it. Changed the subject." James reviewed her behavior during their conversations, and then realized that she was about to join a group for transplant parents. He groaned softly. "Oh, don't tell me." He stared hard at Don. "Did she lose a transplant child?"

"That's for her to tell, if she chooses. You should know better than to ask me."

"It's not as if she's your patient or anything."

"You're all my patients in one way or another. This camp is a place for healing, a place for everybody to deal with their transplant experiences. Why do you think we include the whole family?"

James watched Rachel hesitantly open her chair and position it slightly back from the others. "I don't know, I figured it made it easier for the kids."

"No, it's because everyone in the family is affected by having a sick child, including the brothers and sisters. And because we wanted to give parents a place where they can just be people again."

A place where they could just be people again? James wasn't sure he knew how to be just a man anymore. He'd been the single father of a medically needy kid for so long now that he'd almost forgotten what it was like to deal with his own needs, his own desires.

Don clapped his hands. "Okay, folks, let's get settled so we can start."

James positioned himself beside Don so he could watch Rachel on the far side of the circle. This afternoon she wore a white shirt with patriotic red, white and blue stars across the neckline.

The camp director opened the session by saying they could discuss anything, whether it related to transplants, child-rearing, whatever they wanted. An awkward stillness fell over the group before someone began to talk. Topics ranged from dealing with sibling rivalry to medications. Nolan brought up the unique trials—and joys—of step-parenting a transplant child. His love for Cherish shone clearly in his face as he spoke, and James found himself happy for Michelle, glad that someone had found a mate who could handle the demands of a sick child.

And Nolan had been there, as much as possible, through the whole thing. He and Michelle had started dating about six months before Cherish's heart transplant. They'd married soon afterward. James and Molly hadn't made it to the wedding because Molly had still been in the hospital—waiting. He figured if a relationship could handle that kind of stress, then it should last a lifetime.

Rachel sat still and quiet, slumped in her chair as though trying to make herself invisible. Was she here as an observer, as she'd mentioned the first day? She wasn't reacting to any of the transplant-parent topics as if she'd had a transplant kid herself. Although she'd flinched empathetically when one woman spoke of nearly losing her son.

"You know something I'm curious about," Don said during a lull in the conversation. "How many of you have had contact of any kind with your donor families?"

Rachel straightened in her chair so fast she almost fell out of it.

"I *am* the donor," one mom said, "and I've got the scars to prove it." She rubbed her stomach while others chuckled knowingly.

Part of James envied her. How wonderful it would have been to be able to give Molly what she needed himself. Unfortunately, people didn't come with spare hearts. Kidneys, livers, even lung transplants were being done with living donors, but hearts…they were beyond living donor capabilities.

"That's fantastic, Mia, and I'm sure it was a great relief for you to be able to donate your kidney to Sean. But I wasn't talking about living donors, whom you often know before the surgery." Don scanned the circle of parents. "Anybody here have an experience with an unrelated, unknown living donor?"

Heads shook all around the group.

"So what about the rest of you? Any contact with the cadaveric donor families?"

Rachel gasped, then pressed her hand over her mouth, eyes going wide.

"Rachel? Was there something you wanted to say?" Don asked.

She shook her head slowly, lowering her hand back down into her lap. "No."

"*Cadaveric* is kind of a harsh word, isn't it?" James asked Don softly. He struggled with the image. Molly's heart had been a gift from another child, and James couldn't—wouldn't—picture that child as a cadaver. An angel, yes, a cold cadaver, no way in hell.

"I was counseling people before you got out of grade school. I know what I'm doing," Don said from the corner of his mouth. "Trust me."

"We met our donor family," a man to James's right volunteered. "It was a great chance to thank them in person. I mean, it sounds kinda lame, how do you actually thank someone for saving your child's life? But I think they were really pleased to see how well Paul's doing. I think it made them feel like something good had happened from the horrible accident that took their seventeen-year-old daughter's life."

"Did they ask you to stay in touch?" Don asked.

"We send them holiday cards, and usually an update on the anniversary of the transplant."

"That's nice that they wanted to meet you and be in touch," said the woman next to Rachel. "I sent a letter through the Organ Procurement Organization, thanking our donor family, telling how much I appreciated their gift of life, and how well Olivia is doing now. I sent a picture of her, and told them I'd really love to meet them."

James shifted in his chair. He'd written his own letter to the family of Molly's donor—ended up crumpling up at least a dozen copies before he was satisfied with it. But he agreed with the other father. It just seemed so lame. "Thank you" didn't begin to cover the deep gratitude he felt toward the family of the little girl who'd given Molly a second chance. How did you thank someone for giving your child life when theirs had died?

"And?" Don asked.

"And nothing. I didn't even get an anonymous note back through the OPO."

Neither had James. But he'd just chalked it up to the fact that the donor family wasn't interested in knowing more about them, or having contact with them. He knew everyone dealt with their grief in their own way and he certainly didn't want to intrude.

Rachel murmured something that had the neighboring woman glaring at her.

James leaned forward in his chair. "What was that, Rachel? I didn't hear you."

She lifted her chin and met his gaze. "I said, maybe they weren't ready. Nobody seems to understand that sometimes people just aren't ready."

"Aren't ready for what, Rachel?" Don asked gently.

"To face it, to deal with it..." She lifted both shoulders and let them fall again.

The woman next to her shifted to face her head-on. "Look, no offense...Rachel, is it?"

Rachel nodded.

"I'm just not sure what your credentials are to be part of this discussion. I mean, I know you're teaching arts and crafts to two of the kids' groups, but other than that, why are you here?"

Rachel looked stricken by the woman's words, and as much as he wanted to know the answer to that particular question, too, James couldn't help but want to throttle the tactless lady.

"Come on, girl, tell them," Don murmured under his breath. "Lay your cards on the table."

James shot him a sharp glance, then returned his attention back to Rachel. She had her thumb at her mouth and was chewing on the nail, eyes cast downward at the grass in front of her chair.

"Well?" The busybody in the next chair folded her arms imperiously across her chest, the queen waiting for a response.

His stomach constricted when Rachel briefly looked at him. Not close enough to see for certain, he could guess that there were unshed tears in her eyes. He started to rise, but Don's beefy hand clamped over his forearm.

"Don't. Sit still and hope she pops," Don said softly.

"Credentials?" Rachel asked in a tremulous voice. "You want my credentials?" She turned and glared at the other woman. "A pair of lungs, two kidneys, a liver and a heart. How's that for credentials?"

"I—I don't understand," said Her Majesty.

Rachel jumped to her feet, knocking over her lawn chair. "Dammit, why doesn't anyone care that I'm not ready for this?" she yelled. Visible tremors shook her entire body as she let her gaze slip from person to person around the circle. "My only child, Daniel, my baby, was a donor."

James slid to the edge of his seat, heart in his throat at her revelation. *Oh, Rachel.*

Stunned silence descended upon the group until the only sounds were the chirping birds in the shade-providing trees.

She slapped a hand over her mouth as though realizing what she'd just said, and turned her back on the circle. The woman on the other side of her rose to drape an arm around Rachel's shoulder. Rachel whirled, nearly tripping on the overturned chair, and stumbled into the center of the group. "Don't—don't touch me."

"Tell us about Daniel, Rachel," Don encouraged. "Tell us about your son. We want to hear about him." He looked to the parents for support. "Right?"

Murmurs of agreement floated up from all around the circle.

She shook her head. "No. I can't…"

"You can."

A solitary tear tracked slowly down her right cheek.

James's heart shattered into a thousand tiny pieces for her. It was one thing to live with the fear of losing your child, quite another to deal with the reality of it.

"I have to go," she announced, pinching the top of her nose briefly. "I have to go." She squared her shoulders and lifted her chin, striding quickly toward an opening in the circle. Once she passed the ring of chairs, the facade of decorum vanished. She broke into a trot, then a flat-out run in the direction of the cabins.

James jumped to his feet, only to be stopped once more by Don's grip on his arm. "Let go of me," he said firmly. "This time I'm going to her. She needs someone."

"She does. See if you can get her to talk. Make her tell you about him." The older psychologist released him.

James raced after her, catching a fleeting glimpse of denim and long legs as she dashed around the corner of the main building as though pursued by the devil himself.

Rachel's feet pounded the dirt road as she hurtled toward her cabin, desperately controlled tears blurring her vision. Her stomach churned, and her heart, her heart ached with an intensity she hadn't thought possible anymore.

The screen door to the porch slammed shut behind her as she burst through the cabin entry. Just inside, she crumpled into a heap, the harsh green carpeting burning her bare skin. She rolled onto her side, knees drawn up, and gave the tears free rein. "Oh, Daniel," she sobbed.

Coherent words gave way to animal howls as the carefully constructed walls she'd hidden behind since the loss of her baby gave way. She breathed in jerking gasps, exhaling on a sob. Her nose ran, and tears trickled down into her open mouth, carrying the faint taste of salt.

On the edge of her consciousness she heard the screen door slam, but was too deep into her grief to worry about who was going to find her in this pathetic condition. Her marriage was over, her son was gone, her career threatened. What did it matter anymore?

"Rachel," a deep voice murmured. Warm hands circled her back. "That's it, you let it go."

Strong arms gathered and lifted her, carried her to another place. Soothing words washed over the edges of her brain. She buried her face into James's firm chest and sobbed as though her world had ended.

Time ceased to have meaning.

She'd never known such pain.

Or paradoxically, such comfort.

James held her close and rocked her, his warmth and motion a soothing balm on her raw soul. He stroked her hair, crooned words of encouragement as she continued to flood his shirt with her tears.

When at last she had the strength to lift her head from his chest and look at him, the compassion and empathy in his eyes nearly broke her composure again.

He cupped her cheek in his palm, brushing her final tears away with his thumb. "Better?"

She nodded, but then lifted her shoulders in a shrug. "Tired."

"I'm sorry about your son, Rachel."

The image of his face blurred and she swallowed hard. "Thank you," she whispered.

"Will you tell me about him?"

"I—I need a tissue." She sniffed to illustrate her point. "Oh, look at your shirt."

He glanced down at the trails of moisture, then smiled at her. "It'll wash."

She tried to force an answering smile for him. God knew, he deserved it. Cradled in his arms, she felt safe, protected, comforted. No one had ever held her like this and allowed her to weep all over them, not Roman, certainly not her father.

A new sense of loss washed over her when he gently lifted her from his lap and set her in the corner of the sofa. He climbed to his feet.

"Don't go!" She reached for his hand.

"I'm not." He squeezed her fingers reassuringly. "I'm just going to get you that tissue."

What a mess she'd made of things, not counting his shirt. Now they all knew about Daniel. She'd broken down in front of a group of strangers. How would she face them again?

James returned from the bathroom with a box of tissues and a warm, wet washcloth. "Here, wipe your face. It'll make you feel better."

"Not to mention look better. I probably have

mascara tracks down my face and look like hell, don't I?''

"That's one of those questions a sane man knows not to answer.'' He took the washcloth back from her. ''Here, let me.'' He knelt in front of her, then swiped the cloth across her cheeks. ''There.'' He tossed the wet terry-cloth onto the glass end table.

James lowered himself to the sofa at her side. ''Now, you were going to tell me about your son.''

''I was?''

''Yes, you were.''

''Are you trying to counsel me?''

''Do you think you need a counselor?''

She considered it for a moment. Maybe it was time. ''Probably. But…I think I need a friend more.''

Something ominous, like a thunderhead, crossed his expression, darkening his face for the slightest moment before he inhaled deeply and sighed.

She averted her eyes. ''I'm sorry. That was rather presumptuous of me.''

''No!'' His fingers cupped her chin and lifted it until their gazes met. ''I'd like that very much, Rachel.''

His thumb grazed the underside of her lower lip, setting off sparks deep in her belly. The weight of his gaze on her mouth birthed the irrational hope that he would kiss her. Maybe the pain would go away. Or at least be forgotten for a moment.

"I want…" he murmured.

"Want what?"

"I want—" he lowered his hand "—to help you."

She smothered her disappointment and shifted on the sofa, tucking her feet beneath her legs. She yanked the sunflower pillow from behind her back and clutched it in her lap. Of course he didn't want to kiss her, she looked 'a fright and she'd collapsed like a babbling baby in his presence. Her cheeks tingled as she studied a piece of lint stuck to the black center of the pillow.

"Will you let me help?"

She nodded.

"Then tell me about Daniel," he urged softly.

"How he died?" She hadn't been there at the time of the accident on the playground. It had been Roman's weekend with Daniel, but she'd pictured the scene enough times in her mind. Still, she didn't know if she could actually talk about it.

"First tell me how he lived."

Warmth flooded Rachel's chest as she allowed the memories of Daniel to escape their hiding place. A tiny smile tugged at her lips. "Always on the move. Daniel was all boy. I swear, the only time he relaxed was when he was asleep."

"Must have been hard to keep up with him."

"There were days when I fell asleep about ten minutes after he did."

James groped for the right words, the words that

would help her see how much her bravery in Daniel's death had meant to others. "Molly was rarely like that before the transplant. In fact, there were days when all she did was sleep. Her body just didn't have the strength for being a regular kid."

"Poor thing," Rachel murmured. "She has so much zip now."

"Exactly. And that's because someone out there had the courage, just like you, to donate a beloved heart so my little girl could live, and have a chance to be a kid." He leaned forward and took her hand. "Rachel, what you did was a wonderfully brave and unselfish thing. You and Daniel are heroes. You saved lives."

An ember of fire appeared in her blue eyes. "I wasn't being brave and unselfish, only logical. And you know what? The only life I wanted to save, I couldn't."

"I understand. I felt helpless with Molly, too."

"You *don't* understand." She yanked her hand free and jumped from the couch, hurling the pillow into the corner she'd vacated. "Your child lived! Mine didn't. Why? Do you ever ask yourself that?"

"I do." He rose to his feet but kept his distance from her. "The hardest thing about being a transplant parent is sitting at your child's bed, praying for a miracle, and yet knowing the price for that miracle is the death of someone else's child." They paced the small living room in parallel. "I really am sorry about Daniel, Rachel."

"You want to know the hardest thing about being a donor parent?"

Hell no! He had enough guilt over the whole thing without knowing. But she needed to tell him. "Yes."

"The hardest thing for me was letting him go when he still had a beating heart. I knew in my head he was gone already, but my own heart just couldn't seem to accept it. He was gone, but he didn't look gone. My dad took me to the chapel, and then they took Daniel away. I kept picturing him on a cold operating room table, surrounded by doctors and nurses who didn't know him, who didn't love him." Tears trickled slowly down her cheeks again. "Oh, he'd been declared dead before that, but they needed to keep his heart beating."

So it could be transplanted into someone like Molly.

Though grateful for Rachel's—and all the others' like her—courage, he would have preferred to live the rest of his life without the image of her small son on that operating table while she wrestled with her grief in a lonely hospital chapel.

CHAPTER FIVE

THE IMAGE OF HER LITTLE BOY still haunted him several hours later as he sat before a roaring campfire behind his cabin. Nolan and the girls were out on the road in front, catching lightning bugs in plastic cups, and Tyler slept in a baby seat behind his mother's chair. Moonlight flickered through the trees and frogs honked in a throaty chorus down near the lake.

"Do you ever think about it, Michelle?" James asked, leaning forward in the webbed lawn chair, prodding the bonfire embers with a long stick.

"I wondered when you were going to talk," she said. "Think about what, exactly?"

"The donors. Their families."

"Every day."

"So do I. But not like I did today." James stirred the red coals. "Usually I just think about how wonderful it was for them to help someone else in a time of tragedy. And I'm grateful. And I hope they've found peace with their loss. But today…"

The frogs broke into another throaty refrain, and faint laughter drifted from the front of the cabin, filling the hole in the conversation.

"Today you ran smack into another parent's grief and it scared the hell out of you."

The stick slipped from his hand and dropped into the dirt at his feet. "I can't wait to see your bill for this session," he murmured, bending over to retrieve it. "You know, I don't practice cosmetology, and you shouldn't dabble in psychology."

"Ha! Shows what you know. In my neck of the woods in North Carolina, a beautician is a woman's sounding board, just like the bartender is for the men."

"And here I thought all you women did in a beauty salon was gossip."

"James…" Michelle folded her arms across her chest. "You can't fool me."

Probably not. They'd spent a lot of time together in the hospital when both girls were waiting for hearts. Many cups of lousy coffee and late-night chats had led to a valuable friendship. He'd rejoiced with her when Cherish had gotten her heart, and held her when she'd cried over her daughter's early bout of rejection.

But that didn't mean he wanted to hear her analysis of him.

He glanced over at the next cabin. No lights burned inside, and he could imagine Rachel sitting in the dark, alone, trying to deal with the emotions they'd stirred up earlier. "She didn't come to dinner. Maybe I should go and check on her."

He cracked the stick in half over his knee and tossed the pieces into the fire, then rose to his feet.

Michelle reached for his hand as he passed. "Are you sure that's a good idea?"

"She's dealing with this alone. No matter how bad things got for us, we were never alone. We had a support network at the hospital. I had my parents, you had Nolan. Who does she have?"

"You're supposed to be here for Molly and you, not someone else. On vacation, remember? No psychoanalyzing?"

"She needs a friend, Michelle. Just like we both did at Children's Hospital."

"But do *you* need a friend with that much baggage?"

"We've all got baggage, but some people's is heavier than others'."

He gave Michelle's hand a quick squeeze and released it. "I'll be back in a few minutes. Let Molly know if she comes looking for me, okay?"

She sighed. "All right. But I'm telling you, this is a mistake."

Was it? He pondered while he trudged toward Rachel's cabin. As a psychologist, he knew he could be of assistance. As the father of a transplant kid, he felt a sense of obligation. He might never meet Molly's donor family, but he could express his gratitude to this surrogate. As a man…

That was where he got into trouble.

The memory of her soft curves pressed tightly

against him as he cradled her in his arms provoked a flash of heat.

Maybe Michelle was right. Maybe this was a mistake.

"Dad! Dad! Lookit!"

James turned. Molly hurtled in his direction, white T-shirt easily discernible in the moonlit night. "Don't run in the dark! You'll fall. And don't roll your eyes at me."

Her laughter as she slowed to a trot confirmed what he hadn't seen, but had guessed correctly.

"Lookit." She shoved a plastic cup covered with cling wrap into his hands. "I caught four lightning bugs."

He lowered himself to one knee and studied her offering. The tiny creatures flickered yellow neon pulses from their tails.

"Aren't they cool?"

"They sure are. Are you going to keep them in here?"

"Nah, we'll let them go in a bit. Did you know you can make a wish when you set them free, and if they light up, your wish will come true?"

"No, I didn't. Who told you that?"

"Trudy and Don. That's why they named the camp Firefly Wishes."

He grabbed the end of her ponytail and gave it a gentle tug. "And what will you wish for, Unsinkable?"

"Da-a-ad." She groaned. "First, I'll wish for

you to stop calling me that.'' Then she grinned at him. ''And I'm not telling you what else. It's a secret.''

''Okay.'' James handed his daughter the bug container.

Molly glanced over his shoulder at the nearby cabin. ''Are you going to Miss Rachel's?''

''Just for a few minutes. I want to check on her. She had kind of a rough afternoon.''

Molly nodded. ''I know. I heard about her little boy.''

He gripped her shoulder. ''How did you hear about that?''

''It's all over camp, Dad. Everyone is talking about it.''

James sighed. He did his best to shelter her from stories like that, but she'd seen far more death than any eight-year-old should have.

''Here.'' Molly pressed the cup back into his hand. ''Maybe these will help. She probably needs some wishes.''

''Don't you want them?''

''I'll catch more. There's a bunch of them over in the bushes on the other side of the road.''

''That's very sweet, tiger. You go ahead, because it's almost that time.''

Molly groaned. ''Don't I get to stay up later? It's camp!''

''It's already past your usual bedtime and you

need your rest.'' He gave her a quick hug. ''Go on.''

''All right.'' She scampered off in the direction of their cabin.

''Don't run!'' He shook his head. Kids. They never listened to words of warning.

But then, sometimes neither did their fathers.

The weathered boards of Rachel's porch steps creaked beneath his feet, and the screen door's hinges squeaked. He paused outside the main entrance, tilted his head and listened.

Nothing.

She didn't respond to his rapping, either, so he cracked open the door and took a cautious step inside. ''Rachel? It's me, James.''

Silence, broken only by the rattle of the ceiling fan in her living room. His stomach tightened as her words of the afternoon came back to him. *Dammit, doesn't anyone care that I'm not ready for this?* Had they pushed her too far, too fast?

''Rachel?'' He checked the bathroom first, and loudly exhaled his relief upon not finding her there. Too many possibilities for doing harm to oneself in a bathroom. The bedroom door stood slightly ajar, and he swung it open, his relief complete.

She sat cross-legged in the middle of the bed, clutching a pillow in her arms. He flipped the light switch.

She flinched, blinked hard against the sudden brightness, then swiveled until her back faced him.

Clothes littered the room. Khaki shorts and pastel shirts were draped across the open suitcase on the luggage stand; jeans cluttered the nearby floor. The dresser drawers hung at odd angles, most of them empty, one in the apparent process of being emptied.

"You going somewhere?" He leaned against the doorjamb and shoved his right hand in his pocket, the left clutched Molly's lightning bugs.

"I thought about it."

"I didn't take you for a coward, Rachel. Running won't make the pain go away." The bugs flickered in their makeshift holding cell, iridescent yellow flashes of hope. *I'd wish it away for you, if I could.*

"What will?"

"Facing it is a good start. Time will help."

"How long, James? How long will it take to fill the hole in my heart?"

He didn't dare tell her there'd always be a hole, though smaller than the one now threatening to consume her. "I don't know. How long has it been since Daniel died?"

She rose off the far side of the bed and tossed the pillow at the headboard. "Heading on a year and a half." She rubbed her temples. "Or maybe it's been forever. Sometimes I get confused."

With an empty chuckle, she crossed to the suitcase, retrieved a turquoise blouse and began to fold it. "They sent me for tests, you know."

"Who's they?"

"My father. Jerry. The people who love me."

"Tests?" Now he was the confused one.

"Yeah. Because of the forgetfulness. They did a CAT scan, an MRI, an EEG. Alphabet soup of tests. They thought something was wrong because I was never like that before." The shirt landed in the dresser drawer and she picked up another. "Of course something was wrong! My son was dead."

He set the plastic cup on her night table and moved closer. "Didn't anyone treat you for depression, Rachel?"

She snorted. "Shows what you know, Dr. McClain. Thompsons don't get depressed. They don't take pills in bad times. They lace their combat boots tighter and carry on like good soldiers do."

"No one had to know. Just you. And not all treatments mean pills."

A lemony-smelling shirt wrapped itself around his face, and he clawed at it.

"Make yourself useful and fold that." She straightened the dresser drawer. "I live in a very small town, James. Everyone knows everyone, and their business. The doc wouldn't blab, and probably not the pharmacist, but the bigmouthed women who work in the drugstore are another matter entirely. Why, they're so bad, practically nobody buys birth control in town." This time her laugh had a genuine hint of humor in it. "The condoms there have a longer shelf life than Spam."

James stepped closer to her, offering the folded garment. "That's usually not a good thing."

"Tell me about it." The half smile she gave him faltered, and her lower lip quivered slightly. "That's how I got Daniel."

He put on his best nonjudgmental face, one he'd had a lot of practice with in his office. "So, Daniel was—"

"A surprise! A delightful, wonderful surprise." The final piece of clothing vanished into the dresser and she slammed the drawer shut, then turned to face him. "Why am I telling you this?"

"Because I'm your friend. We established that this afternoon, remember?"

"I have other friends, James McClain. I don't talk to them about this."

"And there's your problem. Which I told you the first night. You can't hold all that stuff inside you without something happening. Like forgetfulness. Or ulcers. Or a bunch of other stress-related illnesses."

"Thank you, Dr. Sunshine." Her blue eyes pleaded for something from him. Reassurance?

"I have something for you."

"You do?"

"Yeah. Actually, it's from Molly. Come outside with me and I'll give it to you." He retrieved the plastic cup from the night table and cradled it in his hands, hiding it from her view. He left the bedroom and headed for the front of the cabin.

"What is it?" she asked from behind him. "Hey, at least give me a hint."

"No hints." He flipped on the porch light as he passed the switch, then led her out the screened door and down the steps. "Okay, close your eyes." He waited a moment. "Are they closed?"

"I don't think I know you well enough to close my eyes."

"For crying out loud, Rachel, just do it."

"Okay, okay. They're closed."

He turned to her. Moonlight flickered softly over the gentle features of her upturned face. Her delicately shaped lips were slightly parted. Moonlight, closed eyes, parted lips… God help him, she looked for all the world like a woman waiting to be kissed.

Suddenly the need to kiss her ignited and burned like a wildfire in a drought-scorched forest. He struggled to subdue the impulse—a kiss was the last thing either of them needed.

"Well?" she prompted.

He cleared his throat. "Uh, here." He closed her hands around the cup. "You can open your eyes now."

As if on cue, two of the tiny creatures flashed in unison. "Oh, fireflies." Her voice caught. "Daniel always loved catching fireflies in the summer."

"Trudy told the girls that if you make a wish and the fireflies flash when you release them, your wish will come true."

She bit down on her lower lip as she stared at the lightning bugs. "If only it were that easy."

"It is to kids."

"Yes. Be good and Santa will bring you what you want, the tooth fairy will swap your lost teeth for cash, and Mommy will kiss it and make it better."

She glanced back up at him and once more a solitary tear tracked down her cheek. His final shred of professionalism slipped away, and suddenly, he was just a man. He longed to gather her in his arms and soothe away all her pain.

"But Daniel didn't live long enough to lose a tooth, and Mommy wasn't able to kiss it and make it better."

"I know." And a kiss from James wouldn't make anything better for her, but dammit, he was tempted to try. "And so you've stopped believing in magic."

"Haven't you? After all that Molly's been through, do you still believe in magic, James?"

"I still believe in miracles. That there's healing in laughter, and in the kindness of strangers. I believe in angels like you…and like Daniel."

"And what about firefly wishes? Do you believe in them?" She held the cup closer to his face.

Between the flickering insects and the dappled moonlight breaking through the swaying trees, he could see her eyes. He saw a tiny spark of hope, and he just couldn't crush it, any more than he could crush Molly's faith in magic. He reached for that unwavering faith of childhood that he'd tried to instill in his daughter, the knowledge that all things were possible. The Unsinkable Molly Mc-Clain. She'd survived against the odds. "Yes," he whispered. "I believe in firefly wishes."

And in that moment, he did.

"Good. Then wish with me, James. There are four fireflies. Two apiece."

"But Molly wanted you to have them."

"You believe more than I do. And I'm sure she won't mind if I share them with her dad." She offered him a quivering smile. "Your daughter is kind and loving, James. You should be proud of her."

"I am."

Rachel removed the elastic band from the cup's rim, and lifted the edge of the plastic wrap. "Ready?"

He nodded.

"Okay."

Barrier removed, the tiny insects crawled to the lip of the cup. The first one flitted into the air and hovered near their heads.

"That's yours! Wish, James!"

I wish healing for your aching heart, Rachel.

As it flew off, the bug's tail light flashed in farewell, and a gentle warmth flooded him.

"You got it. Here go the rest, get ready." She

closed her eyes as the trio launched themselves off the cup.

He held his breath. She scrunched her face tighter with the effort of wishing. He quickly glanced upward. Only one of the little insects flashed.

Rachel blinked rapidly. "Blast, I missed them. Did they flash?"

"Yeah. Yeah, they did." A small lie, but then, it was the believing that was important, right? The power of positive thinking?

"Good."

The relief on her face made him curious. "What did you wish for?"

"I figured unselfish wishes were best, so I wished for other people."

"You did? Who?"

"Isn't there a rule that says if you tell, then it doesn't come true?"

"Not that I know of."

"My first wish was for you and Molly."

"Oh?"

"Yes. I wished Molly's new heart will stay strong and healthy so…so you never know this pain."

His own heart skipped a beat, then tried to crawl into his throat. The hair on the back of his neck prickled. How the hell did he respond to that? She'd meant well, but, damn, talk about hitting where it hurt. He cleared his throat. "Thanks. No parent should ever know the pain of losing a child."

"No," she whispered. "It's just not right. You never expect it."

"What was your second wish?" he asked, seeing the clouds gathering in her eyes again.

"That the parents of Molly's donor would know peace in their loss."

"That's a very good wish, one that I make frequently." He captured her empty hand and gave it a little squeeze. "One I wish for you, too, Rachel."

She lowered her head. "Maybe one day."

"Not maybe. One day you will. It will get easier, I promise. You might not know it, but you made big strides toward that today."

"And how am I supposed to face those people tomorrow? That's why I was packing. I couldn't stand the idea of them looking at me and knowing, feeling sorry for me."

"Hey." He released her hand and lifted her chin with the tip of his index finger until she met his gaze. "Pity and empathy are two different things. You've faced these parents' greatest nightmare."

"What did you wish, James?"

"Me?" Not about to confess his first wish, and having forgotten to make a second, he cast about for something to lighten the mood, something to distract her. "I wished…" He skimmed the underside of her bottom lip with his thumb. "I wished for a kiss."

Her eyes widened. She drew back her head, but he didn't release her. "You did not."

"Did so." Or might have, anyway, had he thought about it. He traced the M-shape of her upper lip, delighting in the silky texture beneath his fingertip. "I very much want to kiss you, Rachel."

Her mouth quivered under his fingers and she shook her head ever so slightly. "I don't think that's a good idea."

"Probably not, but right now I don't really care."

She slipped her palm to his chest and pushed.

He dropped his hands from her face and sighed, struggling to control the urge to dip his head and taste her. "Okay. Then how about breakfast with Molly and me in the morning?"

"Um, I…"

"You have to eat." Instinct told him her thinness had a lot to do with the emotional baggage she carried, not vanity. *How many meals has she missed over the past year and a half?* "You might as well do it with us."

"Maybe." She pressed the empty plastic cup into his hand. "Give this back to Molly so she can catch more fireflies if she wants. And tell her I said thanks for the wishes." She turned away from him and started up the creaky steps to her cabin.

"Rachel?"

She paused, glancing over her shoulder. "Yes?"

"There's no time limit on when firefly wishes come true. I believe I'm going to get mine. Eventually." He winked at her.

The tiny, halfhearted smile she gave him in return made it all worthwhile. "Maybe. Good night, James."

"'Night."

He definitely wasn't good at listening to warnings.

Not even the ones he gave himself.

"SHH." MOLLY PRESSED Cherish back into the bushes across the dirt road from Miss Rachel's cabin. "Here he comes." The girls crouched among the branches, hiding as her dad walked by. He had a weird expression on his face, one she'd never seen before. His eyes seemed wider than normal. Then he shook his head, and his lips tightened into a thin line, like he did sometimes when he wasn't happy with her. Molly covered her mouth with her hand and held her breath until he'd passed. Then she exhaled softly.

"Did you see that?" Cherish whispered. "He was going to kiss her."

"Really? Do you think so?" Molly stood up and danced in place, causing the shrub's leaves to rustle. "That's great! It's working. My plan is working! We need to keep them together somehow. Hey, if they go on that date, maybe I can stay with you while they're gone. Maybe Dad will even let me sleep over in your cabin. Wouldn't that be neat? I've never gone on a sleepover."

Cherish brushed dirt from her knees, then straightened up and stared at her. "Never?"

Molly shook her head. "Grandma's house doesn't count."

"That's horrible." Moonlight glinted off Cherish's short blond hair and her friend grinned widely at her. "We'll just have to get them together. And soon, all he'll be thinking about is Miss Rachel."

"Cool. And maybe then he'll forget about stopping me from having fun."

CHAPTER SIX

EARLY MORNING SUNBEAMS danced through the leaves, and birds chirped as Rachel strolled back up the overgrown path from the mist-shrouded lake. She kicked a rock and sent it skittering into the bushes.

Sleep hadn't come easily the night before, and while she wanted to believe that the majority of her thoughts had been about Daniel and the transplant children she'd met, she had to admit James had taken up way too many of them—far more than his share. Far more than was wise.

Finally there had been the dream.

With James. And the fireflies. And...kissing.

Lots of kissing. Heart-pounding, toe-curling, bone-melting kissing.

Kissing that led to more. Much more...

She shook her head to throw off the lingering effects of the dream, the wonderful jumpy feeling that lodged in the warmth of her stomach.

The reality was that after kissing came sex, which led to surprise pregnancies and unplanned marriages, which resulted in wandering husbands, separations, fathers distracted by their new bimbos…

Her throat tightened. *And terrible accidents.*

She swallowed hard.

She could be forgiven being scramble-brained under the influence of moonlight, fireflies and caramel-colored eyes filled with compassion, but in the broad daylight, Rachel would allow herself no such leeway.

She rounded the corner of the cabin and came face-to-face with the Goat, which only served to reinforce the idea that kissing led to trouble.

Coated in dust from the dirt roads, the car bore only a passing resemblance to the proud, clean, shiny toy that had spent most of its time in the garage. The bushes rustled and a tiny red squirrel darted out, streaked across the road and clambered onto the hood of the GTO. He posed there, a natural hood ornament, whiskers twitching as he rubbed his face with his little paws.

Roman would have had a fit.

What would James say? The thought appeared from nowhere, but she considered it. He seemed to appreciate the Goat almost as much as Roman had. He occasionally even exuded the same smooth self-confidence her ex had.

But last night, Roman would have belittled her hesitation and kissed her, anyway.

Where James had actually responded to her cues

and not pushed. Which made him all the more attractive.

The squirrel darted off the car as Rachel stomped her heel into the dirt. "Trouble, nothing but trouble."

"What's trouble?" Don ambled up the dirt road, strings from his ragged denim cutoffs swinging against his thighs.

She sighed. "Given my life of late, the correct question is 'What's not trouble?'"

He halted in his tracks, eyebrows creeping toward his shaggy salt-and-pepper hair. He nodded at her, one hand caressing his beard. "Wow. That was actually an open, honest acknowledgment of the fact that your life isn't what you want it to be. Good for you."

"Oh, puhleeze. Next thing, you'll be asking me how I feel about that."

"How *do* you feel this morning?"

"Just fine and dandy. Thanks for asking."

Don shook his head. "There goes our honesty."

"People don't want honest, Don, they want comfortable. And guess what? People aren't comfortable when you start blathering on about how rotten your life is, or that your son died and left behind a big hole and you're not quite sure how you're going to make it through another day. When people ask you how you are, they want you to say fine."

"I know about son-size holes in your life. And I know you're not fine."

She studied the chipped pink nail polish on her big toe, then lightly scuffed the dirt with the front of her sandal.

"Rachel?"

She glanced back at him.

"My son was twenty-three when he died. He left behind a wife and a two-year-old daughter. I've been in the place where you are." He paused and ran his hand over his beard again. "But life is about living, and you need to move on. Figure out how best to honor Daniel's memory. By letting life pass you by? Or by grabbing hold of it and squeezing out all you can?"

"I'm trying to carry on." *Like the good soldier I am. Dad should be proud.* She pinched the bridge of her nose.

"You need to do more than carry on, Rachel. But it's a start. A good start." He offered her a pensive smile. "I'm here to help. Do you have any questions for me?"

"Oh, tons."

"Great." His smile widened. "Like what?"

"Like what do you do with this place for the other fifty weeks of the year?" Rachel swept her arms in an expansive gesture to indicate the camp.

Don chuckled. "Okay, change the subject. That's fine. In the summer, we run a number of other programs, not just for transplant kids, although that's our pet project, obviously. We also run programs for AIDS kids, cancer kids and diabetic kids. Then, we do other things—Scout groups, family reunions, even corporate retreats. And Trudy and I shut the place down in October and fly south for the winter.'' He mock-shivered. ''Can't take these winters anymore.''

''That sounds nice.''

''It is.'' Don shoved his fingertips into his pockets. ''Well, I have to get over to the dining hall and make sure everything is running smoothly for breakfast. If you need help with all that trouble, you just give me a shout, okay?''

She nodded.

He turned on the heel of his battered running shoe and started back the way he'd come.

''Don?''

He paused and looked over his shoulder.

''Thanks.''

He smiled and offered her a thumbs-up. ''Just doin' my job, ma'am. And helping out a fellow passenger on the journey.''

She turned back toward the cabin. The nail polish on her toes needed replacing if she was going to wear open-toed sandals all day.

Doin' his job?

Had James simply been doing his job, as well? All the talk of firefly wishes and kissing her, had that been just a psychologist working an emotionally fraught situation?

She slammed the screen door shut behind her.

ALREADY DRESSED FOR breakfast, James dialed his partner, Nicholas Cordova, at home. Without Cord's understanding, James didn't know how he'd have managed with Molly. Cord never minded picking up the slack when James had to be at the hospital. Having their offices only about a half-hour drive from Pittsburgh helped. James had been able, unlike many parents with critically ill kids, to juggle his time with Molly in the hospital and his career. "Hey, Cord. It's me. What's going on at the office?"

"Office?" A low groan rumbled through the phone. "Is this the service? Is this an emergency?"

"It's me, and you know it." James shifted the cell phone to his left hand and pushed the curtain away from the open window, watching Rachel retreat into her cabin following her conversation with Don. Why didn't he have bionic ears? Or at least a spy toy like the one Molly used for eavesdropping when she thought he wasn't paying attention? He desperately wanted to know how Rachel was feeling this morning.

"No, this is not my partner. He knows not to call me at—" a rustling of bedcovers was followed by another low groan "—seven-ten in the morning unless it's an emergency. Since this is not an actual emergency, I'm hanging up now and going back to sleep."

James knew he'd do no such thing, so he launched right into his questions about their practice and some of the patients he was concerned about.

"Enough business," Cord finally grumbled. "You're on vacation, man. You're supposed to be relaxing. Understand?"

"Yeah, yeah."

"How are your friends and their kids? Met any gorgeous women?"

"Michelle, Nolan and the kids are fine." James one-handedly stowed yesterday's dirty clothes in a laundry bag and dropped it on the floor of the closet.

"I noticed you're avoiding the other question, which doesn't surprise me. Besides the fact that you're as dateless as a monk without a calendar, I'm sure that camp is no place to meet eligible women."

"Actually…" The uneven floorboards creaked beneath James's feet as he crossed to the bed. He smoothed the blue-and-white-checkered bedspread. Then he plumped the pillows, squeezing the cell phone between his ear and his shoulder.

"Actually, what, dammit?"

"There is this…woman…."

Cord hooted into the phone, making James pull it slightly away from his ear. "I don't believe it. You go to a family camp and find a woman. Only you, partner. So," Cord chuckled, "tell me about her. She must be something to wake you up after all this time. Beautiful?"

James closed his eyes and pictured Rachel. He didn't dare admit it was her mouth and the way she'd looked in the moonlight last night that really got to him. "She's got a rear that's just…too fabulous for words."

"Aah, sweet. Hair? Eyes?"

"Blond hair, blue eyes."

"Another transplant parent?"

"Actually, she's a donor mom."

Conversation paused for a moment. "Hold it. Back the truck up. A donor mom? As in, she had a kid who was a donor?"

"Yeah."

Complete silence from the other end of the phone made the hum of Molly's hairdryer from the bathroom sound incredibly loud to James. "Well?"

Cord cleared his throat. "How do you feel about that?"

"Shove the counseling and just tell me what you think."

"It doesn't matter what I think. What you think is the important thing. However, since she's lost a kid, maybe she'll understand your obsessive-compulsive behavior when it comes to Molly."

The hairdryer whined to a halt, and James lowered his voice. "I am not OC with Molly."

"Are so. But that's neither here nor there."

"Dad?" Molly stuck her head through his bedroom doorway. "My hair's dry now. You can do it."

James held up one finger. "Be right there, tiger. I'm talking to Uncle Cord."

"Cool. Tell him I said hi." She withdrew from the doorway.

"Molly says hi. I gotta go. I need to take care of her."

"You need to take care of James, too. For once, think about yourself a little. Molly's doing great. It's okay to think about your needs, too."

"Thank you, Dr. Cordova." James applied a heavy dose of sarcasm to the title. "Have you heard from my patient, Rose DeWitt?"

"All's quiet on that front. Her ex has been behaving himself, so she's managing to hold things together."

"Good. You know how to reach me if you need me."

"Yup. Have some fun, bud. Kick back and relax a little." A sharp click ended the conversation.

James sighed. Relax? How was he supposed to relax when he was tied in knots over the woman next door?

RACHEL HESITATED ON THE blue cabin's porch step. The cool morning breeze stirred the chimes, creating a metallic clinking.

Was having breakfast with James McClain a good idea after last night? Did she really want to put herself in that position? On the other hand, James and Molly could act as a buffer against all those other people she had to face this morning, the ones who'd seen her make a fool of herself yesterday afternoon.

Squaring her shoulders, she marched across the porch, drawing to a halt once again outside his door.

"I did not kiss her, not that it's any of your business." James's voice carried through the open front windows onto the porch.

"But Cherish said—"

"I don't care what Cherish said or what she thinks she saw last night."

Last night? Rachel's cheeks tingled.

James groaned. "Maybe we need to establish some ground rules. I, as the father here, will kiss whomever I want, whenever I want. You, as the daughter, will not kiss anyone until you're a heck of a lot older, and then only father-approved boys who are kind, afraid of me and germ-free."

"Eeww, I don't want to kiss some icky boy."

"Thank God" came James's soft mutter.

Rachel covered her mouth with her hand and tried to swallow the laughter threatening to erupt.

"But I don't mind if you want to kiss Miss Rachel. I like her."

A small burst of warmth blossomed in the center of Rachel's chest, but she wasn't sure if it was because Molly had given her father permission to kiss her or because the child liked her. Maybe a combination of the two?

Another masculine groan reached her ears. "I am not having this conversation with my eight-year-old."

Rachel leaned closer toward the window.

"I think it's great, Dad. Does this mean you're taking her on that date?"

"We are *not* going on a date."

A surprising wave of disappointment washed over her, dissipating the pleasant warmth. Not that she intended to date him, but still, that stung. Obviously she'd been right. His wish for a kiss had been a fabrication, a psychologist handling a distraught woman in whatever way he thought would work.

"But what about the dinner you won? You can't waste a whole dinner. And Miss Rachel would be disappointed. She probably worked real hard to keep up with you so you would win."

A bittersweet smile curved the left corner of her lips upward. Molly McClain, champion of wounded women. The child was all spunk.

"Molly, hold still."

"Ow! Dad, take it easy, that hurts!"

"It wouldn't if you'd hold still. Come over here."

"Ow! Stop!"

Through the window Rachel saw James, his hands tangled in his daughter's hair as he pulled her toward the kitchen counter.

A memory from a long time ago surfaced. Rachel

slammed the door into the far wall as she charged into the cabin. "Don't do that. Let go of her hair!"

James paused, one arm outstretched in the direction of the counter, the other hand still clutching strands of Molly's hair.

"I said let her go!"

"If I let go, I'll lose what little progress I've made on this French braid." Amusement sparkled in his brown eyes. "How about handing me that comb?"

"French braid?" Rachel's knees went wobbly and she glanced down at Molly, whose eager face beamed a wide grin at her. "You're braiding her hair?" She passed him the black comb from the counter. *Add ability to French-braid a little girl's hair to the list of amazing things about this man.*

"What did you think I was doing?" James deftly retrieved a strand of hair, then clenched the comb between his teeth and began weaving.

"When I saw you pulling on her hair, it reminded me…" Rachel shook her head. "I—I…never mind."

"You bust into my cabin and I don't even get an explanation?" he muttered around the plastic.

Rachel glanced back at the wide-open door. "I'm sorry. I just thought…"

James plucked the comb from his mouth. "You thought I was hurting her, didn't you?"

"She was yelling ouch."

"You came to rescue me from my mean, hair-pulling father!'' With a giggle, Molly squirmed free from her father's grasp and flung her arms around Rachel's waist.

James threw his hands into the air. "Molly! Okay, that's it. Forget the French braid. Which, by the way, was your idea to start with,'' he reminded his daughter as he deftly undid the beginnings of the complicated braid. "Now you can have a ponytail or pigtails. What'll it be?''

The little girl backed away from Rachel and glanced up at her. "Ponytail, like Miss Rachel's.''

Rachel smiled at the child, the pleasant warmth creeping back into her chest to replace the burning embarrassment she'd felt only moments before. "Definitely easier than a French braid.''

"I'll say,'' James murmured. In a flash, his daughter's hair was styled. "There.'' He glanced over Molly's head. "Have you decided to join us for breakfast?''

Rachel nodded.

"Good.'' James's watch beeped, followed immediately by a chiming from the one on Molly's wrist.

Rachel arched an eyebrow and inclined her head at him.

"Medicine time,'' he explained, going to the kitchen cabinets. "Molly has to take her meds on time for them to work the best. So, we do 7:30 a.m., and 7:30 p.m.''

"Meds?''

"To keep my body from rejecting my new heart." Molly snatched the small plastic cup with the pills and tipped her head back, dumping them into her mouth. She grabbed a water glass from him and washed them down.

"All right, ladies, let's go." James ushered them outside. They strolled leisurely along the dirt road, Molly skipping on ahead.

"You were quite a sight, busting into my cabin like that."

Rachel flushed and ducked her head. "I'm sure I was. I can't seem to do much right these days."

"I think it was very brave of you to intervene." James stopped walking. "But you should know that Molly is my life. I'd never do anything to hurt her."

"I do know that. But…"

"But it looked bad, I'm sure. Who pulled your hair?" He cast her a sideward glance and started walking again, small clouds of dust kicking up around his brown dock shoes in the wake of each step.

She easily matched her pace to his. "A teacher."

"A teacher? What kind of schools did you go to?"

A half smile tugged at her lips. The urge to tell him warred with her normal urge of keeping everything close to herself. "DODD schools."

"Okay, I'll bite. What's a DODD school? Is that like Montessori, only where the teachers pull hair?"

She shook her head. "Department of Defense Dependents. My father was a military man."

"Oh. That explains a lot."

Up ahead, Molly squatted down on the side of the road, obviously fascinated by something she'd discovered in the dirt.

"It does? Like what?"

"Like how you keep everything bottled up inside you. I'll bet emotions weren't shown much in your house, were they?"

"No. We all had to be good, stoic soldiers."

"And how did you father feel about a teacher who pulled his kid's hair?"

The image of her father, dressed in dirt-and-grass-covered cammies, M12 slung over his shoulder as he stormed into her nearly empty first-grade classroom, came back to her clear as day. "He was not pleased. I was scared to death he was going to be furious with me. My mother had called him in the field after the school had called her. All my crying in the background really upset her. Dad made it to the school before Mom. What a sight. He was on maneuvers, and when he came through that classroom door with his gun over his shoulder, I'm not sure which of us was more nervous, the teacher or me.

"Dad believes in discipline, but he also believes in fair play. Luckily I happened to be on the right side in that little misunderstanding. But Dad reminded me that soldiers didn't cry, that I'd worried my mother with my crying.'' And Rachel would give anything for the chance to worry her mother again with her tears. Her mom had died two years before Daniel's birth. Rachel often wondered what advice her mother would have given her about Roman.

''Bet that teacher didn't pull your hair again.''

''Definitely not.''

''Dad!'' Molly came running back down the dirt road in their direction, hands cupped together, arms extended out in front of her. ''Look what I found.''

''What this time, Unsinkable?''

She skidded to a halt, tilted her head to the side and scowled at her father. ''Da-a-ad.'' Her sneakered foot stomped into the ground, creating a large dust cloud, and she jerked her head in Rachel's direction. ''Not in front of other people, remember?''

Rachel pressed her lips together tightly. How could she have ever thought this man, who could do French braids, would hurt his charming daughter? She'd just chalk it up to lack of sleep and too much going on in her life.

''Sorry. Whatcha got?'' James leaned over for a better look.

Molly opened her cupped hands and a toad jumped out, landed on the powdery road, then quickly hopped back into the underbrush. ''Oh, no!''

James shook his head as he straightened up.

"We're on our way to eat. Toads and other critters—"

"Carry germs." Molly sighed and extended her now-empty hands toward her father. "I know, but he was so cute, I just wanted you to see him."

"Not before we eat, okay?" He reached into the pocket of his faded denim shirt and retrieved a small plastic bottle, then squeezed hand sanitizer onto Molly's outstretched palms.

"Sorry," Molly mumbled, rubbing her hands together vigorously.

"It's all right. Just remember to go into the bathroom and wash them when we get to the dining hall, okay?" The recapped bottle disappeared back into his shirt pocket.

"Okay, Dad." Molly skipped off again in the direction of the camp's main building, leaving the adults to amble along behind her.

"Toads aren't high on my list of favorite animals, either," Rachel told him.

"They're not?"

"No, they always pee on you. I'd rather have a snake."

James stopped, causing her to do the same. His eyes widened as he stared at her, then he broke into a devastating grin that eventually grew into a throaty chuckle. "You are just full of surprises, aren't you?"

Rachel lifted her left shoulder, then let it drop.

"*Life* is full of surprises. Some of them are good, some not."

He reached out and tucked a loose strand of her hair behind her ear. "I'd say you qualify as one of the good surprises. You're not what I expected to find at summer camp."

Heat rose in her cheeks, and she fumbled to interpret the glow in his eyes. "What? You mean a donor's mom?"

"No. I mean—".

"Dad!" Molly yelled from the doorway of the main building. "Hurry up! Cherish is already here!"

A wry smile appeared on his face. "That's my daughter, always impatient."

Rachel stifled a sigh, wondering what he really had wanted to say. "I can understand that. We old folks are far too slow for them. Daniel had two speeds—supersonic and warp."

"That's Molly these days."

They entered the main building and turned down the long corridor that led to the dining hall. Molly scurried into the bathroom at the far end, darting back out just as they reached the doorway. She held her hands up and grinned at her father. "Ok, Dad? I'm gonna go say hi to Cherish."

James nodded his approval and began to follow his daughter.

Rachel paused in the entryway. The scents of bacon and eggs made her mouth water, but she hesitated when several people glanced over at her.

She backed up a step but stopped when a large, warm hand slipped over hers.

"Rachel." James squeezed her fingers lightly. "You promised me breakfast this morning. You're not reneging on that, are you?"

"I said maybe."

"Consider me a kid. I think maybe means yes." He pulled gently on her hand. "Come on, you have to eat." His eyes once again conveyed his understanding of her reluctance and he offered his strength through his warm fingers now entwined with hers. "And you have to face them all at some point. Might as well be now."

"Spoken as a counselor?"

"No. Spoken as a friend."

Several slow seconds ticked by while she stared into his eyes, then she squeezed his fingers back. "Thank you."

"My pleasure." A spark glinted in the caramel depths. "Shall we?" He released her and gestured toward the breakfast line.

She nodded and took one step into the room.

The clapping began. First one woman at the closest table, then it spread to those near her. Then the woman rose to her feet.

Rachel froze in place. Surely they weren't applauding her? The scene she'd made yesterday wasn't enough—they were looking for an encore?

More people rose to their feet. She could see their hands moving together, but a roar in her ears blocked out the sounds. Her chest tightened. Trudy's words from her office upon her arrival came back: *They'll consider you a hero.*

Her throat closed and she struggled to breathe. A woman left one of the tables over by the windows and hurried to her, head and eyes lowered as she closed the gap between them. Rachel recognized her as the sharp-tongued woman who'd asked for her credentials and started the whole messy spiral.

"Rachel?" She didn't wait for a response. "Honey, I just wanted to say how sorry I am about yesterday. I had no idea—"

Rachel clenched her hand into a fist, trying to resist the overwhelming urge to pinch the bridge of her nose or better yet, to remove herself from the room as quickly as possible. James gently pressed his hand into the small of her back. Gratitude for his support washed over her. "Thank you." She focused on the woman as she said it, but the words were meant for him.

The woman removed a green ribbon pin from her shirt. Her fingers trembled as she quickly placed it on Rachel's. "I want you to have this. It's for organ donation awareness."

Rachel glanced down. The green stood out starkly against her white blouse. The pin weighed down her heart like a heavy stack of textbooks. "Oh, no, I couldn't—"

"Please. I want you to wear it in honor of your little boy." She grabbed Rachel's hands. "For Daniel."

Unable to speak, Rachel nodded and shook the woman's hand, then whirled and buried her face in James's chest, drawing comfort from his closeness.

He wrapped his arms around her and held her tight. "Easy," he whispered. "It's okay. They're just trying to show you how much they appreciate what you did."

Rachel trembled. She'd done nothing. She was no hero, no selfless person who'd tried to save other people's lives when her son died. She was a complete fraud.

She hadn't wanted to donate Daniel's organs in the first place.

CHAPTER SEVEN

"YOUR FATHER'S LOVE LIFE is none of your business. You're a little too young to be playing matchmaker." Cherish's mom wagged a finger at Molly, then turned to include her own daughter. "I don't know what you two are up to, but knock it off."

Molly glanced over her shoulder, watching her dad steer a pale and slow-moving Miss Rachel along the breakfast buffet. "But he was holding her. I saw it with my own eyes."

"She was upset, Molly. Doesn't your father hold you when you're upset?" Cherish's mom patted Tyler on the back as he squirmed against her shoulder.

Molly slumped lower on the bench. "Yeah. But don't you think he likes her, even a little?"

Nolan chuckled warmly. "Oh, yeah, he likes her all right." His wife's elbow caught him firmly in the side. "Oof. Hey!"

"See, I told you." Cherish smiled at Molly, winked and stabbed another piece of French toast. Golden maple syrup dripped onto the plate as she lifted it toward her lips.

Molly's mouth watered. She darted another quick glance over her shoulder to check on her dad, then returned her attention to Cherish's breakfast. "Give me a bite." She opened wide and leaned in closer. Her friend popped a square of the sweet, gooey stuff into her mouth.

"Mmm." Molly hummed, eyes closed. French toast was just short of heaven in her book. Too bad her father didn't find it nutritious enough. When she opened her eyes, she discovered Cherish's mom giving her a knowing look. Molly silently begged her not to tell. Mrs. Driscoll sighed and shook her head. Molly grinned in response. "Thanks. Guess I'd better go and get my own food now."

She headed off toward the buffet line, wishing for more than one bite of sweetness, but knowing she'd end up eating a gluey blob of heart-healthy oatmeal.

By the time she returned with her tray, her dad and Miss Rachel were just sitting down. Molly slowed as he whipped out a bleach towelette and scrubbed down the table in front of the space beside Cherish, making sure she arrived at the table after he'd finished his embarrassing actions. How was he supposed to impress Miss Rachel when he acted like that? She was going to think he was a nutcase—which in some ways, he was.

"Oh, good, Molly. Here, you sit next to Cherish."

Molly slid into her place, nudging her friend in

the process and rolling her eyes. Cherish tried to stifle a snicker, but ended up snorting like a pig. She quickly covered her mouth with a napkin and they both giggled.

They sat in silence for what seemed like several long minutes. With her spoon, Molly picked at the lumpy oatmeal that clung to the sides of the blue bowl. Scooping up a small portion, she turned it upside down to check the thickness. The blob didn't move, even with a shake to encourage it. This stuff was far worse than the oatmeal her father made at home.

"You're not eating," her dad said softly.

She looked up, the words to defend her finicky behavior waiting on the tip of her tongue, and discovered, to her surprise, that his comment—as well as his attention—was directed at Miss Rachel.

"Oh." The woman looked startled, as if she'd forgotten the food sitting before her. She glanced down at the plate. "Oh," she said again, "I didn't get a knife." She nudged the tray forward slightly. "Or a napkin." A deep sigh escaped her.

Dad jumped to his feet. "Not to worry. I'll get them for you." He brushed his hand lightly over Miss Rachel's shoulder. "You stay here and start on that bowl of fruit. You don't need a knife for that."

Molly waited until he'd left before spearing the final piece of French toast off Cherish's plate and quickly eating it. "Did you like the fireflies last night?"

Miss Rachel looked over at her. "Yes, I did. Very much. I think that was the nicest present anyone's given me in a long time."

A tingly feeling spread from Molly's stomach across her chest. Miss Rachel's pretty blue eyes held hers. "Better than the marshmallow?"

The tiniest bit of a smile started in the corner of Miss Rachel's mouth. "Definitely better than the marshmallow."

"Did you make some wishes?"

Miss Rachel nodded.

"Good. You don't have to tell what they were."

"Thank you."

Molly's dad returned and doled out the knife and napkins he'd gotten. Leaning over the table, he peered into her bowl. "That oatmeal looks more like wallpaper paste." He held out a glass of milk. "Here, Molly. If you stir some in, it should make it better."

"Tastes like paste, too." She made a funny face at him, then accepted the glass from him as he chuckled. "I hope this helps."

"Eat," her dad commanded, first her, then he swung to include Miss Rachel. "You, too. Good health starts with good nutrition, and although I wouldn't call that—" he gestured at the French toast on her plate "—good nutrition, I'm willing to settle for you to eat anything."

"Is that what I have to do to get something good, stop eating?" Molly muttered, stirring the milk into the oatmeal.

"What was that?" Dad asked.

"Nothing."

Cherish's mom handed the baby to Nolan. "Here, take him so I can eat now."

Eyes wide, Molly watched Miss Rachel drown her French toast in the sticky syrup. Her own spoon reluctantly dug into the oatmeal.

A woman in a white tank top came up behind Miss Rachel and laid a hand on her shoulder. "I'm sorry about your son. I just wanted you to know that I admire your courage." The woman patted her, then moved away quickly.

Miss Rachel pushed the plate forward on the tray and sighed.

Dad always said talking about bad things could make you feel better. "How did your son die?"

"Molly!" the other adults at the table chorused. Her father glared at her, and Cherish pinched her thigh under the table. Molly kept her attention on Miss Rachel.

Rachel locked eyes with the little girl across the table, the protests and gasps of shock from her adult tablemates ringing in her ears.

"You apologize right now, young lady!" James admonished.

"No," Rachel said.

"No?" He cocked his head and raised one eyebrow.

"No. She doesn't have to apologize. She asked the one question you all want the answer to." The weight of their stares made her stomach quiver, but it was Molly's eyes, a hazel just a shade darker than her father's, that Rachel focused on. There was no pity in those sparkling eyes, only the natural curiosity of a child.

She inhaled deeply and folded her hands on her lap. "It was the first nice spring weekend. Daniel's dad took him to the playground. There was a big, wooden structure shaped like a castle, and he loved going there. But he climbed somewhere he shouldn't have, and he fell and hit his head."

"Did it hurt? Did he cry?"

"I wasn't…wasn't there, but no, I don't think he cried. And I don't think he felt anything." At least, that was the belief she clung to. She needed to believe there'd been no pain for him. "His brain was hurt too badly, I think."

"And that was why he died? His brain was hurt too bad?"

Rachel's throat tightened, and she wrung her hands beneath the table. Mist gathered, obscuring her view of the somber freckled-faced child across from her. She lowered her gaze and nodded.

Warmth tingled the skin of her left thigh as James's fingers skimmed its surface, and then he latched on to her hand beneath the table and squeezed it hard.

She squeezed back.

The small island of silence at their table was surrounded by an ocean of happy chatter and occasional laughter. Only the baby stirred at their table, wriggling and cooing in his father's arms.

"Wanna trade breakfasts with me?"

"What?" Rachel's head popped back up and she looked across the table again, blinking to rid herself of the stubborn tears.

Molly's eyes twinkled at her. "Trade. You eat my oatmeal, I get your French toast." She darted a quick glance at her father.

Rachel pushed the tray toward her. "Go ahead, you can have it. I'm not very hungry—"

"Absolutely not!" James released her hand and retrieved her tray. "Molly's just pulling your leg. And you are both going to eat, and I mean now."

Rachel opened her mouth to protest, but he pressed his finger against her lips. "No excuses. Now eat."

He dragged his fingertip across the fullness of her lower lip as he pulled his hand away, igniting a slow smolder that had nothing to do with hunger. For food, anyway. Those concern-filled eyes remained fixed on her mouth as he reached for her fork. "Open," he ordered.

Of its own accord, her mouth obeyed, and he

slipped the fork past her lips. Sweet syrup and cinnamon.

A sweet man and a spunky child.

His intense gaze on her mouth.

There was no moonlight to blame this time, but all she could think of was the last time his eyes had been on her like that, and his wish for a kiss.

Michelle coughed loudly, drawing Rachel's attention back to the table. "Cherish, you're finished, right?" The older girl nodded. "Okay, let's go. Nolan, give me the baby, then you can take our trays."

Rachel snatched her fork from James's hand and bent over her food, cheeks heating at the direction of her thoughts. Obviously those thoughts had been clear enough that the other woman had been able to see them.

"We'll catch you later, Jimbo," Nolan said, slapping James on the shoulder as he rose to pick up the trays. "You playing in the pool tournament this afternoon?"

"I am. And you're going down."

Nolan chuckled. "We'll see about that." He headed off toward the garbage cans. Cherish followed him. Michelle gathered scattered baby supplies into a diaper bag with one hand.

"Dad, can I go, too? Maybe Mrs. Driscoll will French-braid my hair for me before activities start." Molly grinned at Rachel, then offered a saucy wink.

Rachel forced her lips together, hard. A smile

now, with a mouthful of French toast, would be a messy thing.

"You have to—"

"All gone." Molly held her bowl upside down to demonstrate.

"Go." Her father waved. "But stay with Cherish, and I'll check to make sure you're at your first activity on time."

"Yeah!" Molly bolted from the table, tray in hand, following after her friend. "Cherish, wait! I'm coming with you."

"Good luck in getting her to hold still for the braids, Michelle. I'd advise you just to say no and leave her with a ponytail."

"I know what *I'm* doing, James." As Michelle leaned over to brush a kiss on his cheek, Rachel caught a whiff of baby powder. Her chest tightened with longing and she reached out to caress the baby's chubby knee. Soft baby skin, like silk, met her touch, and Tyler kicked his legs.

"I know what *I'm* doing, too, Michelle."

"Just checking."

In seconds, James and Rachel were alone at the table. Again.

"Well," Rachel said. "Looks like I've done it again. Cleared the table." She watched Michelle sashay out the door. "I don't think your friend likes me very much."

"It's not that she doesn't like you…" James began.

"Then what is it?"

He leaned closer and whispered, "She's worried about me getting involved with you."

Oh, God. Forget food. Rachel swallowed the lump in her throat. "And...are you?"

"Am I what?" His fingers found their way back to her face, he cupped her chin with one hand, and the index finger of the other brushed at the corner of her mouth.

"Get...getting involved with me?"

He moved his head away from hers. "Well, *involved* is such a strong word. We're friends, right?"

She nodded.

"Although, there is that matter of my wish last night...." He touched the edge of her lip. "You're sticky again."

"It's not marshmallow this time."

He inserted the tip of his finger into his mouth, closing his lips around it.

Rachel was sure the heat scorching through her body was going to set the wooden bench on fire, and before they knew it, the whole camp would go up in flames. That would look great in the report to Jerry, wouldn't it?

She watched, captivated, as he removed his finger from his mouth.

"Nope. Not marshmallow. Syrup." He quickly glanced around the room, and lowered his voice further. "And I want..."

"What?"

He hesitated. "To kiss you. God help me, I still want to kiss you."

A whimper lodged in her throat. God help them both, because at the moment she'd like nothing more than to make his firefly wish come true.

Unbelievable.

She'd lived in the shadow of Daniel's death for so long that she'd forgotten what it felt like…to be alive.

Maybe Camp Firefly Wishes really was a place of miracles.

Suddenly she caught sight of a flash of orange.

She backed away from James. His eyes widened in surprise as she groaned.

"What?"

"Trudy and Don are staring at us." She smiled weakly at them. Trudy smiled in response, but Don folded his arms across his chest and squared his shoulders, reminding her very much of her father. "I don't believe it."

"Believe what?"

"All these kids, all these people around us, and I let you make me forget all about them. Blast!"

"So? It's not like we actually kissed or anything. I doubt they'll fire you or anything."

"Fire me," she whispered, then sighed heavily as the reality of her situation thundered back to her. At the moment, Don didn't look like a man inclined to give her a great report. "They might not, but…"

"But?"

"Never mind." She rose from the table. "Thanks for the breakfast company."

"That's what friends are for," he called after her as she beat a hasty retreat.

Good soldiers also knew when to fall back and form a new line of defense.

CHAPTER EIGHT

"YOU'RE IN MY WAY." Nolan nudged James with the large end of the pool cue.

"What?" James glanced at the table and discovered the cue ball resting near the rail right in front of him. "Oh, sorry." He stepped back, swung his own cue around and set the rubber tip on the floor.

The steady *tink-katink* of ongoing Ping-Pong games filled the sunny rec room, and around three other pool tables were several other parents who'd entered the tournament this afternoon. Although, the so-called tournament had quickly disintegrated into individual games with no semblance of organization.

James found it hard to focus on the game. Instead, his thoughts were zipping back and forth in time with the Ping-Pong ball behind him.

What the hell had he been thinking this morning in the dining hall? The urge to kiss Rachel, to lick the sticky smears from her pink lips had been overwhelming, and he just couldn't figure it out. Okay, so she was pretty, and sweet, and damn it to hell if she didn't just twist his heart with her quiet, stubborn strength in the face of her loss....

But almost kissing her with all those people look-ing on? If he didn't know any better, he'd claim to have lost his mind. But he did know better. People who thought they were crazy generally weren't.

So how did he explain the whole thing?

"It was brave of you to let Molly sign up for the bungee jumping. You know, Cherish really wanted to do that, but that was where Michelle drew the line."

Instant panic, icy hot, speared his chest, then spread. Moisture slicked his palms. "Bungee jump-ing? What the hell are you talking about?" James snapped his head up to glare at his friend's grinning face. "Bastard," he mumbled low enough for their ears only. "You are one sick bastard, you know that?"

Nolan roared with laughter. "I had to get your attention somehow. You've got it bad, Jimbo."

"That obvious, huh?"

"A blind person could see it, it's that obvious."

James groaned. "Great." Raising his shoulder, he wiped a bead of sweat off the side of his face. Humid air hung heavy in the room as the old wooden ceiling fans worked hard to create a small breeze.

Nolan leaned over the table, lining up his next shot. "Eight ball, side pocket." He pulled back the stick and let fly. The cue ball kissed the edge of the eight ball, sending it neatly into the pocket. "It is great." He laid the stick on the table. "I win. Third time in a row. You want to concede defeat, or shall I rack 'em up again?''

"I'm not a glutton for punishment." James turned and replaced his cue into the rack on the wall. "Which is why this is a bad idea."

"Playing pool?''

"Playing, period.''

"Oh.'' Nolan nodded wisely. "You know what they say about all work and no play, Jim?''

"Yeah, it makes Jack a dull boy.''

"Wrong." Nolan slipped alongside him, replacing his own cue and the chalk cubes, and dropped his voice. "It makes James a love-starved man. It's about time you found a woman to light your fire again.''

"Great, between you and Cord, I've got two cheerleaders in favor of this.''

"You talked to Cord about it? Wow, I guess it's even more desperate than I thought.''

"Let's get out of here. It's stifling. Maybe there's a breeze outside.''

"Lead on.''

James blinked against the bright sunshine as they headed out the doors. Laughter came from the soccer field across the road as a group of kids played under the watchful eyes of several counselors. James and Nolan strolled in the direction of the lake.

"Molly loves it here. She's having a lot of fun.

I'm glad you guys could be here, too. She's missed Cherish.''

"Cherish has missed her, too, but I gotta tell you, I'm just as happy not to see your face every weekend anymore. No offense to you, but I got tired of the hospital.''

"I hear you. I love Children's and all the doctors and nurses, but I'd just as soon never set foot in there again.''

"Which won't happen, with their biopsies and whatnot.''

James sighed. "That's the truth. And that's exactly why I can't get involved with a woman. Any woman.''

"Involved? Who said anything about getting involved?'' Nolan bent to retrieve a flat rock from the sand and skipped it out across the lake, six hops before it sank beneath the surface. "Didn't you ever have summer romances, Jim?'' He grinned. "Short term, no strings, and they leave you with the sweetest memories for the rest of your life.''

Memories? The memory torch planted firmly in the sand at the beach entrance caught his attention, its flickering flame spouting black smoke into the heavy air. Memories of finding Rachel—had it been only yesterday?—lying on the floor of her cabin flooded him. "She deserves more than that, Nolan.''

Arm cocked back, Nolan paused, then lowered

his hand. "Aah. Is that how it goes? Maybe you ought to let her decide what she wants."

"And even if she does? How do I manage it with Molly?"

"Why don't you start with that dinner you won?" Nolan chuckled. "How I wish I could have seen the race. But I was busy." A rich timbre accented the final word and Nolan waggled his eyebrows. "And there's your first clue. You find time when the kid is busy doing something else."

"The dinner. Molly's been ragging me about that. She says I can't disappoint Rachel."

"So don't. Take her out, have a few glasses of wine, enjoy yourself. You remember how to enjoy yourself, don't you? I wonder if she does?"

Hmm. James wondered that himself. She'd been through so much. "And what do I do with my daughter while I'm off enjoying myself?"

Nolan sent another rock skittering across the lake surface. "She has a sleepover with Cherish, naturally." Blond hair glinted in the sun as he shook his head. "Do I have to teach you everything, Jim? 'Sakes, Cherish has a sleepover at a friend's at least once a week if I have any say in it." He grinned.

The idea had merit, and it certainly was tempting. The very image of a seminormal, grown-up evening glimmered before him, a candlelit dinner with a pretty lady, maybe hold her close and dance... maybe more?

Was he Super Dad? Or was there still part of him that was just a man?

It could be exactly what Rachel needed, a chance to get away from the camp and all the reminders of transplants and her lost son. But did he dare leave Molly alone for the night? It wasn't as if he were leaving her with her grandparents while he worked with patients, this would be leaving her behind for a purely selfish reason.

No, not selfish. For her. For Rachel. "I'll think about it."

Who knew summer camp had such temptations for grown-ups? He certainly hadn't expected to face a dilemma like this. Was it time to think a little bit about himself?

RACHEL LIFTED HER PONYTAIL off the back of her damp neck, wishing she had a few bobby pins to keep it up.

Splashes and laughter drew her attention to the Olympic-size swimming pool where lessons and a game of tag appeared to be in progress. Maybe she could dangle her feet in the water, cool off a bit.

Entering the fenced-off area, she reached down and shucked her sandals, gathering them by the toe loops. The damp concrete was blessedly cool beneath her bare feet. The sharp scent of chlorine hung in the air, and Rachel wrinkled her nose as she scanned the area for the best place to dip her feet without getting in the way.

Off in the corner, tucked in a chair beneath a large umbrella, Molly McClain cradled a hardcover book on her lap. She blew at a stray strand of hair trailing down her forehead, then glanced from her book to the pool and all the splashing kids from her group. Pure, undisguised longing filled her round, freckled face. Her shoulders pulled upward slightly, then slumped back down in an inaudible sigh.

Rachel diverted her steps toward the little girl, who was looking decidedly unspunky at the moment. "Hey."

Molly looked up. "Hi."

"How come you're not swimming with the rest of the group? Forget your bathing suit? I did." Rachel dragged another chair over and dropped down into it, sandals clutched in her lap.

"No." This time the sigh was audible. "I'm not allowed."

"Not allowed? How come?"

"Germs," Molly mumbled.

"Germs?" Rachel sat up straighter. "I can smell the chlorine from here. What germs could survive that?"

The little girl lifted one shoulder and let it drop. "Ask my dad. I'm not allowed in public pools since he saw some story on the news about germs that can live in them, even with chlorine." She brushed at the strand of hair now glued to her forehead with beaded sweat.

Rachel's heart went out to her. "What is it with your father and germs?"

"Remember those pills I took this morning?"

Rachel nodded.

"Well, they make it easy for me to get sick. My body doesn't fight my new heart, but it doesn't fight germs too good, either. All transplant kids have to be careful."

Careful she could see, but obsessive? "I see a bunch of transplant kids in that pool right now."

"Tell me about it." Molly shoved a bookmark into her book and thumped the heavy volume closed.

"I guess that means you can't even put your feet in there, huh? That's what I was going to do."

"Nope."

The droopy expression on the normally sunny face tugged at Rachel. This child was supposed to sit here and watch everyone else have fun? That was just too cruel. "When is swimming over?"

"Next activity is at four o'clock. Nature hike."

Rachel glanced at her watch. It was 2:24. That meant Molly had to sit here in the heat for more than an hour before the rest of the kids climbed from the pool. "Tell you what, why don't you come with me instead of sitting around here?"

"Where are you going?"

"I was thinking about heading back to my cabin to pin my hair up off my neck, and then I'm going to find some other way of cooling off." Hopefully that bag of balloons she'd used for a science experiment was still buried at the bottom of her teaching bag. She didn't recall taking it out, but that didn't mean anything these days.

"Like what?" Molly asked, her face brightening slightly.

"Oh, I don't know. I guess you'll have to wait and see. What do you say?"

"I say, what are we waiting for?"

"Then let's tell your counselor that you're going with me and get out of here." Rachel slipped on her sandals.

On the way out the gate, Molly reached for Rachel's hand.

Rachel's heart skipped a beat, then thudded against her chest as she wrapped her fingers around the child's smaller ones. She quickly chased away the dull ache, the empty void that grabbed her. Life moved forward, and so would she. She had to, or lose what she had left.

Molly grinned up at her.

Rachel smiled back and squeezed the little hand tucked inside hers.

JAMES TRUDGED UP THE DIRT lane toward his cabin. Even the birds had gone silent in the heat of the afternoon, but as he got closer to the end of the lane, he heard muffled shouts and…laughter? A few high-pitched giggles were punctuated by rough chuckles, rusty laughter that sounded like the person was out of practice.

"Got you!" an exuberant voice proclaimed.

More laughter followed, laughter that sounded more natural this time.

Wait a minute. He recognized that voice and the giggles. They belonged to his daughter—who was supposed to be with her group at the pool, not here. James picked up his pace, striding around the side of the blue cabin. "Molly, what are you—"

"Dad, look out!"

A flash of yellow hurtled inches in front of his face. James stopped abruptly. "What's going on here?"

Molly stepped out from behind a bush. Straggly, drippy hair framed her face, and her pink T-shirt clung to her chest. Her formerly white sneakers and socks were spattered with dirt. In her hand, she hefted a round blue object. "We're just having a water balloon fight. Wanna play?" Molly smiled sheepishly and extended the balloon in his direction.

"We?" He scanned for the other culprit, the source of the rusty laughter, and saw no one. He turned back to his daughter. "You're wet! Why aren't you with your group?" James snatched the water balloon from her hand. "Where did you fill these?"

"It's my fault. Don't be mad at her." Across the small glade, Rachel stepped from behind the corner of her yellow cabin, one hand held in front of her, one snaked behind her back.

"Do you realize that she's all wet now?"

"That was the idea, yes. We were just trying to cool off since she couldn't go in the pool."

"She can't go in the pool for a reason! Where did you fill these balloons?"

Rachel crossed the open area between them, stepping around spattered pieces of colorful latex. "Calm down. We used the tap water. No big deal."

James whirled on his daughter. "Molly, you get inside, get those wet clothes off and jump in the shower. Look at you. Your legs are filthy."

Molly's lower lip trembled. "I'm sorry, Dad." She turned and ran toward the cabin.

James jammed his hand into his hair. "Molly, honey," he called after her. "Wait!"

She skidded to a halt, then slowly pivoted on the rubber tip of her sneaker.

"I'm careful because I love you."

She balled her fists and propped them on her hips. "Sometimes I think you love me too much!" Her muddy foot pounded into the ground. "Maybe it's a good thing I *don't* have a mom, because with two parents like you, I'd really smother!" The screen door slammed as she raced inside.

A slow ache built inside him. Smother? Was he really smothering her? No. He had her best interests in mind. Her health. But it hurt to hear her say he loved her too much.

How could you love a person too much?

He took a step in the direction of the cabin but stopped at the touch of a warm hand on his elbow.

"Let her go. Give her a chance to cool off."

James inhaled deeply, then exhaled forcefully.

"I don't understand the big deal. It was tap water." Rachel's soft voice drifted across his shoulder.

"Tap water can be contaminated, too. Not to mention when you mix it with mud..." He whirled to face her...

And forgot Molly's harsh words.

Rachel's white blouse bore the evidence of his daughter's good aim, the moisture rendering it transparent in the bright sunshine. Lace-cupped curves beckoned from beneath the material.

He curled his fingers toward his palms, the urge to touch her so strong pins and needles shot clear up to his elbows.

She stepped closer and her aroma further addled his senses, the faint scent of lemon mingled with the healthy smells of sunshine, water and woman.

Suddenly he was grateful for the weight of his denim shorts, which although hot, hid his erection a lot better than canvas or parachute shorts would.

"You just sent her inside to shower in that same tap water. How much sense does that make?" she asked gently.

He lifted his gaze from the swell of her breasts and locked on her eyes, trying to clear the hormone-induced haze from his mind. "What? Same water?"

"Why did you bring Molly here, James?"

"So she could have a normal summer, have fun."

"We *were* having fun until you came on like a bulldozer." She reached up and tucked a loose strand of hair behind her ear.

The gesture made her breasts jut forward and James bit back a groan. If she moved like that again, even denim wasn't going to contain him.

"I haven't laughed like that since…"

He jerked his head up, caught the fading light in her blue eyes. Something tightened deep in his chest, something that had nothing to do with hormones or lust. He reached out to brush his finger across her cheek. "Since Daniel died?"

She nodded.

"You should do it more often." His fingers glided over the damp, smooth skin of her face, traced the shape of her jawline. "You're very pretty when you smile. And God knows you deserve some fun and laughter."

"What about you, James? When's the last time you did something fun, something impulsive?" She caressed the back of his wrist, rekindling the pins and needles sparking up his arm.

"You mean before now?" He snaked his hand around her waist and drew her against him. She gasped, dropping the water balloon from her hand. It plopped onto the ground next to them.

She tilted her head back, and he dipped his head to take possession of her mouth.

He meant to go slow, easy, but at the first bit of pressure, she parted her lips for him, and he accepted the invitation, deepening the kiss, slipping into her mouth with the tip of his tongue.

Butterscotch. She tasted of butterscotch. He probed deeper.

RACHEL MOANED softly into his mouth. His tongue teased and explored, driving rational thought far away. He slipped his hand lower on her spine. Fingers splayed across her bottom, he pulled her closer, against the hard ridge of his arousal.

He wants me.

The knowledge caused a surge of power to rush through her, a heady feeling of desirability and femininity. Intoxicated by that and the overwhelming heat generated by his mouth on hers, and by his erection jammed against her belly, she whimpered her distress when he pulled away from her.

Only their heavy breathing filled the supercharged air hanging between them.

''Damn,'' he finally whispered, fingers finding her face again. ''I'd say I'm sorry, but I'm not. I guess firefly wishes really do come true.''

''Maybe we should have Molly catch more tonight?''

He cupped her chin. "But now that I've had a taste of your sweetness, I'm going to wish for more than a kiss, Rachel." His pupils widened. "A lot more. Do you understand me?"

Oh, God. She understood, all right. Trouble. Big trouble. Get-pregnant-get-married-get-hurt trouble. And yet, the idea of losing herself in his arms definitely had appeal. He'd sent her halfway to heaven with one kiss. What would he do if she gave him a chance? She swallowed hard. "I…I hear you."

"Don't look so horrified about it. You'll damage my fragile ego." He leaned in closer again, wrapping his arms around her in what could pass for a casual hug if not for the sensual awareness between them. "Nothing will happen if you don't want it to."

Did that guarantee include not getting pregnant?

His warm breath against her ear sent tingles racing up and down her spine.

"I want to know everything about you, Rachel Thompson." He released her and stepped back, tugging on the hem of his polo shirt. Two damp spots indicated where her breasts had crushed up against him. "What do you say we claim that prize we won and have dinner together Friday night?"

Damp spots? Rachel glanced down and heat scorched her cheeks. No wonder he'd come on to her—she looked like an absolute hussy, a renegade from some bar's wet T-shirt contest. She folded her arms across her chest. "Are you asking me on a date?"

His face paled in response to the question. He looked as if he'd swallowed one of the water balloons. "A date? I—um—well..."

Rachel recalled his early morning, adamant words to his daughter, words to the effect that he wasn't going to date her. *Serves him right. Let's see him squirm out of this.* She smiled. "I think that's what they generally call it when a man asks a woman out to dinner."

"Then I guess I am," he said. "Friday night."

"Friday night." She nodded. "It's a date."

CHAPTER NINE

A DATE. JAMES STARED at himself in the bathroom mirror and wiped the last trace of shaving cream off the edge of his face with a hand towel.

He'd lost his mind.

Weeks of therapy would be required to regain it—but he couldn't count on Cord's help, because his partner would applaud the behavior.

Amazing how a man's reasoning ability went to hell the second all the blood rushed south of the beltline. At least, that's what he'd kept telling himself. Far easier to believe it had been the wet shirt and what was beneath it that had gotten him into trouble rather than the ache he'd seen in her eyes when she'd spoken about not laughing since Daniel's death.

He reached for the after-shave bottle propped on the sink, wincing as the lotion bit into his skin.

"Mmm, that smells nice, Dad."

James turned to find Molly leaning against the door frame, the mischievous twinkle back in her hazel eyes, her cold-shoulder treatment of him after the balloon incident obviously over. "What are you up to, Unsinkable? You have your things ready to go to Cherish's for the night?'' His gut tightened at the thought of leaving her for the whole night.

Grinning widely, she shook her head. "Not yet." She pranced in the doorway. "This is gonna be so cool, Dad. Thank you so much!" In the space of a heartbeat, she'd flung herself at him, wrapping her arms around his middle, pressing her cheek against the bare flesh of his stomach.

He gently stroked her unbound hair, a surge of warmth kicking him in the center of the chest. The love of this amazing child should have been enough for him.

Then why did he keep feeling so drawn to Rachel?

"You're the best dad in the whole world."

Yesterday he'd smothered her, and today he was the best dad in the world? "Remember that the next time I tell you to do something you don't want to do."

Molly giggled and tipped her head back to glance up at him. "Okay, right *now* you're the best dad in the whole world."

"That sounds more like it." He released her, spun her in the direction of the door and playfully swatted her behind. "Get your things together. We have to be out of here in about five minutes to get you down to Cherish's so I'm back in time to meet Rachel."

"Ooh, Dad's going on a date." She giggled again as she vanished out the door.

"It's not a—" He stared at his freshly shaved face in the mirror and sighed. "Okay, okay, it's a date." He reached for his toothbrush. "Hey! Come back here. You forgot your toothbrush, you little monkey!"

When Molly returned, he dropped to one knee. She reached for the toothbrush, but he held tightly to it. "Are you sure you're okay with this, Unsinkable?"

She rolled her eyes. "Going to Cherish's? Of course—"

"No. I mean, with me going on a date."

"Oh, Daddy." She looped her arms around his neck and dropped her forehead against his. The soft scent of her hair rose around him. No longer the sweet smell of baby shampoo, but a floral fragrance. "I want you to be happy. You take care of people at work and me at home. You deserve a bunch of dates if that's what you want." She pressed a kiss to the tip of his nose.

Eyes closed, he wrapped his arms around her and held her tight, the steady thump of her heart against his chest a reminder of the treasure—the miracle— she was. "I love you, Mol."

"I love you, too, Daddy." She wriggled in his arms and pushed away. "Now, get a shirt on or you're gonna be late."

She snatched the toothbrush from his hand and dashed from the bathroom once more.

A few minutes later he checked his watch again,

then pulled a cotton polo shirt from a hanger and yanked it over his head. "Molly? You ready?"

"She's ready, are you?" Nolan asked from the bedroom door.

"What are you doing here?" James tucked the bottom of the shirt into his jeans.

"I'm here to pick up Molly and make sure you get off okay." Nolan glanced over his shoulder. "And I've brought you something." He entered the room and held out his hand. "Take this."

James glanced down at the pager cradled in Nolan's palm. "I don't need that, I've got my cell. But thanks."

"Trust me, you need this. Take it." Nolan pressed it into James's hand.

The weight didn't feel right. James hefted it in his palm, then turned a quizzical glance to Nolan, who grinned, and popped open the mock pager.

Revealing several condoms.

James shook his head. "Getting a little ahead of ourselves, aren't we?"

"Hell, no. This is your night, Jim."

"I don't think so." His hormones protested, but he didn't want to expect that the night would land him in Rachel's bed. He still hadn't decided if that would be a smart move or not. Besides, there was no guarantee she'd even consider it.

"A good Scout is always prepared."

"I was never a Scout."

"Shut up and take them. If you don't need them,

then you can give them back. I'll be happy to make use of them.''

James cast a sidelong glance at Nolan. ''Just in case something does get going, and Rachel should happen to ask, just how old are these condoms?''

''How old?'' Nolan's brows bunched in the center of his forehead. ''Why do you need to know that?''

''Because if they're older than Spam, I'm out of luck.''

''Huh?''

''When did you get them? Before Tyler?''

''Hell, no. These are fresh, pal. I bought a nice big box before we came on this trip. Michelle's still nursing Tyler, so this is about it as far as birth control goes.'' His buddy made a slicing motion across his neck. ''And she'll kill me if I get her pregnant again too soon.''

''Too soon? You planning to add another one?''

Nolan's grin turned sheepish. ''I sure hope so. There's a big gap between Cherish and Tyler, naturally, but I'd like for Tyler to have a little brother or sister, too.''

''That's…nice.'' James shoved the plastic pager into his back pocket, feeling slightly envious. He'd always wanted a large family, three or four kids. ''Come on, I'll get you Molly's meds.''

The girls were waiting near the front door when James and Nolan entered the main room. ''I'm giving Nolan your meds, Mol. You have your watch, right?''

''Yeah, Dad, I have my watch.'' She held up her wrist and grimaced at him as he pulled the plastic containers from the kitchen cabinet. ''I have my toothbrush and my pj's and my clothes for tomorrow. I'll remember to take a shower and put on clean underwear. I won't eat any junk food, and we'll go to bed at a reasonable hour. Did I forget anything?''

''Seven-thirty,'' he told Nolan, shoving the small plastic bag into his hands. ''Directions are on the labels, and Molly knows the drill, too.''

''We're familiar with the routine, Jim.''

James turned to Molly. ''Sounds like you've got it all covered. I think you only forgot one thing.''

''What's that?''

''My good-night hug and kiss. I guess I'll have to have them now.''

She dropped her backpack to the ground and entered his wide-stretched arms. He stroked her hair for a moment, then bent over so she could place a loud kiss on his cheek. '''Night, Daddy.''

'''Night, tiger. You be good.''

''You have fun.'' She smiled at him. ''And make sure Miss Rachel has fun, too.''

''I'll do my best.'' He turned toward Nolan. ''You have my cell number, and the number of the restaurant.''

''We'll be fine, Jim. Do make sure you both have

fun.'' Nolan gave him a final wink before he ushered the girls out the door. ''See you at breakfast.''

The screen door slammed shut.

Silence.

The emptiness of the cabin washed over him, and he inhaled deeply. He had a whole evening ahead, an evening when he was to forget about being a dad and concentrate on being on man.

He pulled his cell phone from its holder on his belt and opened it. Yeah, it was working.

A light tap sounded at the door. ''James?''

''Rachel.'' He glanced at his watch and hustled onto the screened porch. ''Sorry, we got a little behind with getting Molly—''

He stopped midsentence and stared. ''You look great.'' The turquoise of her sleeveless blouse set off her sunshine hair and bright blue eyes, and the tight denim capris she wore set off everything else.

Including his hormones.

A pretty flush rose in her cheeks. ''Thank you.'' She gave him a quick once-over before dropping her gaze. ''So do you.''

Okay, now they had the awkward complimenting stage over with. So far so good. He fished for the SUV keys in his pocket. ''Our reservations are for seven.''

She dangled a set of keys from her index finger. ''I thought we'd take the Goat. And I thought you might like to drive.''

He slapped his hand over his chest and groaned.

"Be still, my heart. You're not teasing, are you? It's not nice to tease a man, you know."

"I'm not teasing." She tossed the keys at him.

"A beautiful woman *and* a muscle car." He threw his head back and grunted. "Testosterone overload, here I come."

God, it felt good to be just a man.

RACHEL BLINKED A FEW TIMES as her eyes adjusted to the dimly lit restaurant. Red-and-white-checked tablecloths covered the tables; flickering candles spilled melting wax down their wine-bottle holders. Soft instrumental music swelled in the background, and Rachel tried to swallow the dry sand in her mouth.

Butterflies—or maybe Molly's fireflies—flitted in her stomach as James took her elbow.

What would they talk about now that the car topic had been exhausted? Small talk had never been her forte.

"Right this way." With a smile, the young hostess clutched the menus to her chest and headed toward the back of the restaurant, weaving through the mostly unoccupied tables.

The kitchen door opened as they passed, and the scent of freshly baked garlic bread wafted out. Rachel's stomach did a somersault. She stumbled.

James steadied her. "You okay?"

"Fine." She shrugged off his hand, squeezed her lips together tightly, and followed the hostess.

After they were seated at a secluded table in a little back alcove and had placed their drink orders, Rachel studied the menu intently.

"What looks good to you?"

You do. But she didn't dare voice that opinion, even though it might have distracted her from the memories the little Italian place was threatening to bring to the surface. "I don't know. What are you going to have?"

"I'm not sure. Maybe the lasagna."

"No!" The plastic menu holder clattered against the tabletop and Rachel folded her hands in her lap.

"You have something against lasagna?"

Sweat beaded on the back of her neck. "Sorry. No, you go ahead and order what you want." She could handle it. *For pity's sake, get a grip. It's just food.*

He set down his menu and held out his hand expectantly.

Tentatively, she unwound the linen napkin and placed her hand in his palm. Warmth infused her as he closed his strong fingers around hers.

"Rachel, friends share. They don't bottle things up." He winked at her. "Remember what I told you happens when you bottle things up?"

Yes, you end up looking crazy and incompetent and on the brink of losing the only thing you have left. Only he'd put it more professionally. Something about ending up with a stress-related illness. She sighed and nodded.

"So tell me, why don't you want me eating lasagna?"

The dim lighting, soothing, soft music and warmth from his hand made her feel safe. "What do you call it when a person won't eat something because it made her sick once?"

"A conditioned taste aversion?"

"I have one of those to lasagna."

He studied her intently, and she squirmed in her seat.

"It has something to do with Daniel, doesn't it?"

She bobbed her head slightly. "It was his favorite. I was making it for him—" She cleared her throat. "I had a batch in the oven, cooking, when Roman called to tell me Daniel had been hurt."

"Oh, God." James squeezed her hand. "I'm sorry, Rachel. Okay, no lasagna." He glanced around the restaurant. "Are you sure you want to stay? Because we can go someplace else. We don't have to have dinner here."

"And lose our prize?" She shook her head. "No, we worked hard for this dinner, and Molly cheered us on. Just so long as we stay away from the lasagna…"

"You know, you can recondition yourself. You just have to pair the noxious stimulus with something pleasant." He lifted her hand and placed a light kiss in the middle of her palm. "Something pleasurable." His mouth caressed her skin again.

Heat rushed from the spot where the tip of his

tongue teased gently to flood her entire body. If anyone could recondition her, it would be this man, this compassionate, tender, sexy man. "Really? How does that work?"

His lips pressed against her wrist and she prayed he couldn't feel her heart racing. "Well, you could take it in small steps. If, for example, you found you could tolerate being in an Italian restaurant and smelling lasagna, then you could move on." His chair grated against the floor as he moved closer. "Then maybe you could try having someone eat it in front of you. Eventually you'd be able to eat it yourself."

"What—what about the other stimulus? You know, the pleasurable one? What would you choose for that one?"

"That depends," he murmured, reaching to tuck a stray piece of hair behind her ear, then brushing the backs of his fingers over her cheek.

"On what?" she whispered.

"On whether or not we were alone."

She swallowed hard. "And if we were?" Holy mother of pearl, she was playing with fire.

He leaned over, his words hot on her ear. "Pleasure is so personal, Rachel. What's the most pleasurable thing you can imagine me doing to you?"

Her breathing went shallow, and her eyes closed as thoughts of his large, gentle hands—and mouth, oh, yes, his mouth—all over her body sent a thrum of desire rushing through her bloodstream.

"Mmm, yeah," he whispered. "Whatever that idea is, I'd love to oblige."

And she'd love to let him...if only she—

"Are you ready to order now?" The waitress set their drinks on the table in front of them.

Rachel jerked away from him, face scorching. Hopefully the dim light wasn't enough for either James or the waitress to notice.

James smiled at her and squeezed her hand.

She'd totally forgotten he was still holding it. "I'll...I'll have the lasagna."

His smile faded. "You don't have to do that, Rachel. I mean, what I was saying is correct, but it takes time. It's not just a one-shot attempt. I want you to enjoy yourself tonight."

"Lasagna was always a favorite of mine, too. I want to do this."

James shook his head. Damn, if half his patients had the courage of this woman, his job would be a lot easier. "Are you sure?"

She nodded.

He turned toward the waitress. "The same for me."

They completed their dinner orders, and he sighed with relief when the waitress left them alone again in the dark corner. The flickering candlelight revealed apprehension in Rachel's blue eyes.

"You can still change your order. I can call her back."

"No. This is something I have to do."

"You are a remarkable woman, Rachel Thompson. Brave."

Her lips pursed together, and she shook her head. "Hardly."

"Totally. Coming to Camp Firefly Wishes was an act of courage."

"Yeah, right." She removed her hand from his and lifted her water glass, taking a sip. "It was an act of desperation, not courage."

"I don't understand. Explain it to me." He wanted to know everything about her, from her childhood in a military family, to what she was like as a teacher, to the exact image that had flashed through her mind when she'd closed her eyes and started breathing faster as he'd whispered in her ear.

Especially that image.

She broke off a piece of Italian bread and buttered it. "I was kind of…coerced into coming to camp. In all honesty, it wasn't something I wanted to do."

"Because you weren't ready?" He spread butter on his own slice of bread, watching her from the corner of his eye.

"Exactly." She offered him a slight smile. "It's nice that someone finally understands."

"I understand, but I think you're underestimating yourself. Maybe you were ready but were afraid to admit it to yourself."

Just as he didn't want to admit to himself how

drawn he was to this woman, and not just on a physical level.

"Why would I be afraid?"

"Maybe you feel that starting to deal with Daniel's death means losing him all over again."

"Is that your professional opinion, Dr. McClain?"

"Actually, yes." He leaned back in his chair, waving his slice of bread in the air. "But I have to remind you, we're not on a consultation here. We're—" he swiveled his head, checking for listeners, and dropped his voice to an exaggerated whisper "—on a date."

Her smile widened. "Yes, we are. I'd nearly forgotten. Of course, it's been so long since I've been on a date, you'll have to excuse my rusty skills."

"I hear you." He chuckled softly. "Care to compare? I'll bet mine are rustier."

"Really?"

Mouth full of bread, he nodded.

"I thought a guy like you would have plenty of dates."

"A guy like me? What's that supposed to mean?"

Running a finger along the woven edge of the basket, she looked down, and her cheeks flushed. "I don't know. You're kind of…" The final word of the sentence was mumbled under her breath.

He propped his elbows on the edge of the table. "What was that?"

"Smooth. A ladies' man."

He straightened up in the chair, puffing out his chest. Damn, there was a hell of a lot to be said for a testosterone rush. Who needed drugs or alcohol when hormones could do such a job? "I know you don't mean that as a compliment, but that's how I'm taking it." He chuckled. "My partner would be on the floor, howling. The truth is my last date was about four years ago. And the only reason I remember is because Molly was four years old."

"Four years? Okay, I win. My last date was six and a half years ago. Too bad my husband didn't stop dating at the same time." She propped her chin in her palm, eyes taking on a far-away look.

"He cheated, huh?"

A flicker of hurt flashed in the blue depths as she nodded. "I shouldn't have been surprised, given the reason for our marriage. And talk about a ladies' man? That was Roman to a T. I guess I always hoped he'd change. You know, he missed out on having a dad in his house growing up, and I believed him when he said he wanted to try to make our marriage work." Her dry chuckle sounded forced. "Although, I think maybe Roman's real motivation was the possibility of my father—or Jerry—tearing his head off."

"Jerry?"

The waitress returned with their salads, and Rachel fell quiet until the woman left again. James stirred red vinegar into the mixed greens. "Who's Jerry?"

"Jerry's my principal. And Roman's uncle. He was not happy when he found out there was a baby on the way before a wedding." She toyed with the croutons in her salad. "I could have lost my job. I didn't have tenure at that point, and the board of ed definitely would not have approved of a pregnant, unmarried teacher."

"So he offered to marry you?"

"Eventually. With a little encouragement. But we were the ones who made the final decision."

Over their salads, Rachel explained how Roman had been summoned for a meeting in her father's den—a den she described as the ultimate male retreat, complete with gun cabinet and mounted hunting trophies. When he'd arrived, Rachel had been seated on the couch, and both her father and Jerry were present. After a brief interrogation, as Rachel termed it, the two older men handed the younger one a packet containing two plane tickets to Las Vegas along with hotel and wedding chapel arrangements, all prepaid.

"And that's how I ended up a married woman. Roman and I discussed it, and decided it really was the best thing for all of us, for the baby, for me and my career. I guess it just didn't work out for him the way we expected."

"Did you love him?" A burning sensation developed in the pit of his stomach while he waited for the answer. *Too many peppers in the salad.* He pushed his not-quite-empty bowl away.

A pensive expression filled her face. "I believed I was in love with him. Like many women, I thought my love could change him, heal him." She sighed. "But I don't think I really understood what love was all about. Love is about sacrifice, and sticking around, and working things out. Love is being there through the hard stuff. My pregnancy was the first hard thing we faced, and I thought that since we passed that test, we'd be okay." She smiled softly. "That's enough about me. Tell me something about yourself."

"Well, you're right about love being about standing together through the hard stuff. Tiffany, my ex-wife, didn't get that, either. Our marriage had been smooth sailing until we found out about Molly's heart defect in the second trimester of the pregnancy." His abs tightened, and he tried hard to brush aside the anger that still lingered.

Rachel's fork fell to the table, and she reached for his hand. "Then what happened?"

"Tiffany's first instinct was to ask the doctor if it was too late for an abortion." He squeezed her fingers.

Rachel's mouth gaped open for a moment, then she snapped it shut. "I...I don't know what to say."

"Neither did I."

"Obviously you managed to convince her otherwise."

"Yes, thank God." He couldn't imagine life without the child who'd stolen his heart from the moment he'd first found out about her existence. Even at the ultrasound that had revealed the defect, he'd seen her—a baby sucking her thumb—as *his child,* counting on him to make everything right for her. "But Tiffany didn't understand unconditional love. All she understood was that our baby ended up getting far more attention than she did, and that it was hard work to spend your days at a hospital bedside."

"So she left you and Molly?"

James nodded.

"Her loss." The vehemence in the normally soft voice surprised him. "Molly is a wonderful child, and I can't imagine how a mother could turn her back on any child, let alone one with such a sunny personality. Does she have visitation rights?"

"Only on paper. She lives in California now and doesn't have time for her daughter. Molly's lucky to get a card on her birthday and Christmas."

"That's awful." Genuine concern filled her expression. "Your daughter is a special kid, James. She's lucky to have you for a dad. And your ex obviously got out of line when they were handing out maternal instincts. God, I'd give anything…"

Candlelight glinted off the tears welling up in her eyes. She withdrew her hand, tossed her napkin onto the table and gathered up her purse. "I have to go to the ladies' room. If you'll excuse me..."

He rose to his feet with her and laid a restraining hand on her arm. "Don't be gone too long. I'll be lonely without you."

Eyes downcast, she nodded.

"And I will come in there after you, if necessary."

She glanced up at him through her long lashes, mouth still clenched in a tight line, and nodded again. Shrugging off his hand, she strode quickly across the restaurant. Several other diners, particularly the men, looked up as she passed their tables. A quick stab of jealousy pierced him.

I'll be lonely without you? He sank back down into his chair. And jealousy? What the hell was that all about?

CHAPTER TEN

"WHAT DO YOU THINK THEY'RE doing on their date?" Molly asked Cherish, as they both leaned over the baby in the middle of the bed. Molly reached out and tickled his foot.

"Having dinner, I guess. I mean, that's what they went for."

Tyler cooed at them, making spit bubbles.

"Eewww, look at that!" Molly wrinkled her nose. "Slobber is dripping down his neck."

Cherish laughed. "Beats it dripping down *your* neck, which happens if you're holding him." She took a cloth from a nearby bag and wiped him.

Tyler turned his head away and screamed.

Molly's mouth dropped open. "Wow. He's pretty loud, isn't he?"

"Yeah, he sure is."

The baby made his hands into fists and squished up his face, turning bright red. He grunted.

"Oh, no." Cherish moved to the doorway. "Mom? Come get dribble-puss. He's making a present for you."

A horrible smell drifted from Tyler, who suddenly stopped squirming, relaxed and looked a whole lot happier. "Oh, man!" Molly pinched her nose shut. "How can something so small smell so bad?"

Cherish's mom came into the room and picked up the baby and the diaper bag. "You get used to it."

Molly exchanged a glance with her best friend, who also pinched her nose shut and shook her head.

"You do not," Cherish whispered as her mom left the room with the baby. "That's the worst part about him."

Molly let go of her nose and sighed. "I still say you're lucky. I wish I had a baby brother." She threw herself down on Cherish's bed.

"First you need a new mom for that."

"I know. And that's probably never going to happen."

"Don't be so sure. My mom always said she'd never get married again, but she did." Cherish picked up a cotton ball from her dresser and dumped some alcohol on it, dabbing at her ears. Her pierced ears.

Something else Cherish had that Molly didn't stand a prayer of getting. "I wonder how Dad's doing with Miss Rachel? Is he acting like a dork? Do you think he'll kiss her?"

"Maybe. I dunno."

Molly rolled onto her stomach and propped her chin in her palms as she watched Cherish finish caring for her ears. "Do you think they could end up like people in the movies—you know, fall in love and get married?''

"Then you'd have an evil stepmother like Cinderella had?''

Molly giggled. Sometimes they joked about Nolan being the big, bad, evil stepfather, but really he was a great guy and Cherish loved him. "No, goof. I mean like we get to be a real family and we all live happily ever after. I'd have a mom to do things with, like makeup and stuff. Dad freaks out if I even want to polish my nails.''

Her wristwatch beeped and Molly rolled off the bed. "Meds time.''

Out in the living room, the phone rang.

"How much you wanna bet that's my dad, checking up on me?'' Molly headed for the door with Cherish behind her.

"No way. I'd lose, for sure.''

"We need to catch more fireflies tonight, Cherish. I need more than a distraction for my dad. I need to wish for a new mom to help permanently.''

A new mom who didn't mind a transplant kid and liked water balloon fights.

A new mom like Miss Rachel.

"CAUGHT YOU,'' RACHEL SAID as she slipped back into her chair.

James returned the cell phone to its holder on his belt loop before he looked over at her. Her eyes were slightly puffy and tinged with red, but otherwise she looked fine. "Caught me what?"

"You were checking up on Molly, weren't you?"

"Guilty."

Rachel tsked and shook her head. "Don't you trust your friends to take care of her? How is she?"

"She's fine. Annoyed that I called, but fine." He studied her intently for another minute. "What about you?"

"Me? I'm fine. Why wouldn't I be?"

"Do I need to give you a list? Do I need to remind you again about keeping things bottled inside?" While she'd been gone, he'd asked the waitress to postpone bringing their food, until he was certain she was going to be able to handle it. Knowing how important maintaining her composure was to her, he didn't think falling apart in Giordano's Italian restaurant would be good for her.

He wasn't going to be much good for her, either, if he couldn't keep his mind off how much he wanted to sweep her into his arms, kiss her into a stupor, and then make love to her.

"You're nothing if not persistent, Dr. McClain." She fussed with the napkin on her lap.

"Don't call me that. I know how you feel about my profession, and besides, I told you, I'm off duty tonight. Tonight I'm just James, out on a date with a pretty lady who I already consider a friend. And I wish she'd feel the same about me."

A slight smile touched her lips, but it didn't reach her eyes and barely activated the smile lines around the corners of her mouth. ''You could never be just James.''

''No?''

''No. You're too special to be just anything.''

An intoxicating rush stormed him that had nothing to do with the glass of merlot he'd been sipping. Special. She thought he was special.

He was treading deeper water than he'd expected. Hormones and lust were a helluva lot safer.

Because he thought she was pretty special, too.

He cleared his throat. ''Thanks.'' A ringing cell phone saved him from anything further on that topic line. A brief flash of panic dissipated as he realized it wasn't his.

Rachel pulled a small phone from her purse. ''Hello?'' Her brows knit together. ''Hello?''

When no one answered her, Rachel looked at the caller ID. Blocked number. She stabbed the off button. A quiver ran along her spine.

''Who was it?'' James asked.

She shrugged. ''Nobody, I guess.'' She stuffed the phone back into her pocketbook, unable to shake the feeling that it had been Roman.

She glanced around the restaurant. ''Where's our waitress? I'm starving.''

''Okay, if you're sure.'' James signaled the waitress. ''Now, why don't you tell me what brought you to Camp Firefly Wishes?''

Rachel grappled momentarily with the decision to tell him, then shared the story of Jerry and her father ''encouraging'' her to attend the camp.

His eyes never left her face. If nothing else, the man was a great listener—but then it went with his job.

Didn't it?

The waitress arrived, setting plates of steaming lasagna in front of them and replacing their empty glasses with full ones. The scent of sauce mingled with garlic from the bread wafted to Rachel's nose and she forced down the overwhelming sense of dread that accompanied the smell.

She straightened her spine and firmly grasped her fork, poising it over the plate. ''Okay, I can do this.'' She glanced across the table. Did she dare ask him? The delightful teasing they'd engaged in earlier certainly would help make the food go down a lot easier. Besides, teasing and flirting didn't mean she was about to jump into bed with him.

''Where's that other stimulus you promised? The pleasurable one?''

One side of his mouth curved slowly upward. ''We're not alone, but I'll see what I can do.'' He took her left hand and turned it palm up on the red-and-white-checked tablecloth. His fingertips traced swirling patterns over the sensitive skin, wandering up over her wrist, back to her palm, to the ends of her fingers.

Rachel closed her eyes and sighed. It had been

so long since she'd been touched in any way, not counting hugs from children. She craved adult human contact. His contact especially, she realized with a jolt.

The scent of lasagna grew stronger and she opened her eyes to see James holding a loaded fork. "You ready for this?"

She opened her mouth, and he eased the food in.

Her heart thudded against her chest, and her throat threatened to close off, preventing her from swallowing. She shut her eyes again and prayed not to embarrass herself.

The fork clattered onto the plate and James moved closer, his fingertips leaving her hand and slipping onto her thigh beneath the edge of the tablecloth. Warmth caressed her ear as he spoke softly. "I still don't know what that pleasurable image was you pictured earlier, but I'm game for later if you are."

The image returned, only this time with far more detail: skin-to-skin contact between their naked bodies; James's sensual mouth lingering over her lips, her breasts, her…

A wicked, wonderful sensation crawled over her.

In an effort to clear the lump in her throat, she swallowed the lasagna without tasting it. She opened her eyes to find him watching her intently. "You're game for later? Isn't that kind of risky without knowing what I pictured? What if my image involved tying you up and having my wicked way with you?''

Heat flared in his eyes, and he grinned at her. He tightened his fingers around her leg. ''A man can always hope.'' His eyebrows moved up and down and a rich chuckle rumbled in his throat. ''But you don't strike me as a dominating type.''

''No?''

He shook his head. ''And I'm usually pretty perceptive about those kinds of things. Personality assessment goes with my job.''

''So how do I strike you?'' She accepted another mouthful of food from him.

''You strike me as a very sensual, sexy lady, someone whose idea of pleasure would be *my* pleasure to indulge.''

Sexy? He thought she was *sexy?*

Even Roman's seduction had been more or less the result of a self-challenge to see if he could corrupt Miss Goody Two-shoes. And he'd made it plain a few months into their marriage that he'd found her boring in the bedroom, that even his expert tutelage couldn't make her into something she wasn't. One of her acts of defence after the divorce was to buy herself a whole new set of lingerie.

''I see doubt in those beautiful blue eyes,'' James said, offering her more food. ''I mean it. You became one of my fantasies the moment we met.''

"Fantasy?" she managed to choke out. "Really?"

He pressed his lips together tightly, as though suppressing a grin, and nodded. "With Molly and work, I have neither the time nor inclination these days for much more than fantasy. And, lady, let me tell you, if the reality is half as good..." His eyes darkened, and his cheeks flushed.

She felt pretty flushed herself.

No one had ever fantasized about her before.

The reflection of the candlelight in his eyes illuminated a smoldering that had nothing to do with the flickering flame.

Oh, yeah. Her initial assessment of him had been right. Trouble. And for once, inviting trouble didn't seem such a bad idea.

THE FIREFLY FLICKERED as it flew off into the darkness, and Molly shut her eyes tight and wished again. Hard. The same wish she'd made five times already.

Please, please, let my dad fall in love with Miss Rachel so she can be my new mom.

"Here." Cherish dropped into the dirt alongside the bottom porch step where Molly sat, and handed her another plastic cup. "I got three more."

"Okay, thanks." The cling-wrap lid crinkled as Molly set the fireflies free and wished again. Only one of the fireflies didn't blink his tail light.

"You wanna do something else now? I'm tired of catching fireflies."

"You think that's enough wishing?" Molly stuffed the plastic wrap down into the cup. "I really want to be sure it takes."

"Heck, yeah. Hey, at your birthday you only get one wish. I think you're ahead."

"All right. What should we do now? Wanna go play with your mom's makeup?"

"Nah." Cherish rose to her feet and brushed dirt from her shorts. "I know. Let's go spy on my mom and Nolan."

Molly giggled. "Think we'll catch them kissing again?"

"Probably. They can't keep their hands off each other. At this rate, I'm going to end up with a bunch of brothers and sisters. Maybe next time it'll be a girl."

"Eewww. I still can't imagine anyone actually doing...you know...*that*. Gross." Molly followed Cherish around the front corner of the cabin, bumping into her when her friend stopped suddenly.

Cherish clamped her hand over her mouth, but laughter came out around the edges until she drew in a deep breath and snorted. She bent over, trying hard to smother the noise.

"What's so funny?" Molly whispered.

"You. You want your dad to fall in love with her, you want a baby brother or sister. How do you think you're going to get one? Jeez, grow up."

Molly poked Cherish in the side. "I'm trying to. Dad doesn't even know that I know where babies come from."

"Yikes. Don't you dare tell him I told you." Cherish put her finger across her lips and waved for Molly to follow her. They snuck around to the back of the cabin, peeking around the corner toward the blazing fire in the pit. Cherish's mom and Nolan were cuddled together in a double folding chair, his arm draped around her shoulder.

"You can't blame him, Michelle. It's been a long time."

"I know. It's just that…" Cherish's mom sighed. "I don't know. On the one hand, I feel badly for Rachel. I mean, I've faced the fear of what happened to her. I know she needs someone to love her, maybe even another child, something to help fill the hole in her heart."

A tingle ran across the back of Molly's neck. Miss Rachel needed another child? Cool. They both needed each other. Her wish could help them both.

"But I'm also worried about James. He doesn't need the complications this woman could introduce into his life. And Molly's."

Nolan nuzzled Cherish's mom's hair. "Can't you accept that he just wants to have some summer fun?"

"James doesn't believe in casual fun." She emphasized the last word.

Molly stifled a giggle. That was the truth. She

loved him to pieces, but fun wasn't exactly Dad's big thing.

"So, maybe it's about time he learned. He's a big boy, 'Chelle, so just smile and stop thinking about it."

"I suppose you're right. It's just I know how much Tiffany hurt him, and I don't want to see him get hurt again."

"You can't wrap him in Bubble Pak the way he tries to do with Molly. Pain is an unfortunate part of life, something we all have to deal with from time to time. He just needs to live a little. Maybe if Jim learns that, he'll lighten up on his daughter."

In the dark shadows of the cabin's edge, Molly's eyes widened. She hadn't known Nolan was on her side about that kind of thing.

"How he raises Molly is his business, Nolan."

"And so's his love life, 'Chelle." Nolan pulled Cherish's mom into his arms. "I'd rather concentrate on our love life."

"There they go again," Cherish whispered into Molly's ear as Nolan kissed her mother.

"Don't they ever, like, bump teeth or something?" Molly angled her head for a better view. Sure beat watching kissing scenes in the movies.

"Nah, they've had plenty of practice."

Molly tried to imagine her dad kissing Miss Rachel in the same way. Would he ask her medical history first? Maybe spray her with disinfectant spray? Force her to gargle with Listerine to kill the germs? She giggled.

The kissing couple broke apart and Cherish's mom glanced over the back of the chair in their direction. "Girls? Are you over there?"

Cherish elbowed Molly in the ribs. "Now you've done it."

"All right, you two, show yourselves. I know you're over there."

"Uh, yeah, Mom, we just didn't want to disturb you." Cherish led Molly to the fireside.

"My, how considerate of you." Cherish's mom struggled forward in the sloped seat, her drawn eyebrows clearly showing her disbelief.

"That's us. Considerate." Cherish elbowed Molly once again. "Right, Molly?"

"Uh, yeah, sure. Considerate. Totally."

"I thought you girls were busy making firefly wishes?" Nolan asked, also sliding forward on the double seat.

Cherish shrugged. "Been there, done that, got bored."

"Bored, huh?" Nolan picked up a stick and poked the fire, sending a flurry of sparks upward.

They both nodded.

He prodded the fire one more time, then laid the stick on the ground alongside his chair. "Well, we have this perfectly good campfire, and I hate to see it go to waste. How about I tell you some stories?"

"What kind of stories?" Molly asked.

"The only kind you tell around a campfire," Nolan answered, slipping off the chair to sit cross-legged in front of the fire. He tipped his head downward and looked up at them, the fire casting weird shadows over his face. "Spooooky stories."

Tyler's cries echoed out the open window from the Driscolls' bedroom. Cherish's mom stood up. "That's my cue to leave." She slapped Nolan lightly on the shoulder as she passed. "One hour. And if they can't sleep tonight, you get to stay up with them."

"Yes, hon," Nolan called after her. "Whatever you say, dear."

The girls giggled.

"Sit down, you two. Be sure to stay close enough. Don't want the bogeyman to get you."

Despite the warmth from the fire, a shiver crawled up Molly's spine as she plunked herself down in the dirt in the circle of flickering light. She leaned over to her best friend and whispered, "You're so lucky. Nolan's cool."

"Hey, no whispering over there. Are you ready for a story?"

They both nodded.

"Did you ever hear the one about the monkey's paw?" Nolan's voice dropped down low on the final words.

"Ooh, no," Molly said. "Tell us."

"I don't know, it's pretty scary. I don't want to

end up with you girls camped in my bedroom to-night.''

"Tell us, tell us," they begged together.

"All right, if you're sure." Nolan began the story, voice spooky.

Another shiver crawled up Molly's back. This had to be the best night of her life. Now, if things were going as well on Dad's date with Miss Rachel, she'd really be a happy camper.

CHAPTER ELEVEN

HE COULDN'T WAIT FOR THE meal to end.

Distracting Rachel from the painful memories triggered by the lasagna was driving *him* to distraction.

To still their trembling, James tightened his fingers around her thigh, resisting the temptation to stray a little higher.

She inhaled sharply and froze in place, save for her widening eyes. Her pupils dilated, all but obscuring the blue of her irises.

He swallowed hard and completely stilled himself.

"James." Rachel's voice held a breathy note of desire. Her body shifted slightly forward, pressing against his hand.

He unglued his tongue from the roof of his mouth. "Damn, Rachel." His heart pounded. He removed his hand from her leg and gripped the edge of the table till his knuckles turned white.

She sighed, disappointment filling her eyes.

He swallowed a groan. "Rachel, if I don't get my hands off you, I'm never going to be able to walk out of this restaurant. You still might have to walk in front of me.''

"Really?''

He nodded.

"Oh.'' Wonder and amazement rang in her whisper, leaving James to ponder what kind of idiot her ex-husband had been to make her so question her potent sensuality.

"You sure made short work of this lasagna.'' The waitress scooped up the empty plates. "Now, what can I get you folks for dessert?''

The tiny shake of Rachel's head told James all he needed to know. He wanted to shout with joy. "Nothing, thanks. Just the check.''

"That's all been taken care of. You folks enjoy the rest of your evening and the rest of your time at Camp Firefly Wishes.'' The young server tossed James a saucy wink, then walked away.

"I'm sure we will.'' He dropped a few bills on the table. "Shall we go?''

"Oh, my God. Oh, my God! Henry!'' A woman's frantic voice carried from the front of the restaurant. "Help! Oh, please, someone help him!''

James's chair rocked back and forth on its legs as he jumped up and dashed into the main dining room. A gray-haired woman wrung her hands, standing over a still form on the floor.

James dropped to his knees beside the man. "What happened?'' he asked, fingers already searching the man's neck for a pulse.

"I…I don't know. One minute he was fine, the next minute, he winced, rubbed his arm and fell over. Oh, help him, please!"

"Somebody call 911!" James yelled at the other diners and staff who had already gathered. "Tell them we've got a cardiac arrest." Recertified in CPR every year like clockwork, his training kicked in automatically.

He was vaguely aware of Rachel's attempts to comfort the distraught woman, but soon everything slipped away from him as he focused on the task at hand. Sweat beaded across his forehead and the back of his neck as he alternated fifteen compressions with two puffs of air.

The muscles in his lower back strained in protest.

Eternity passed—in counts of fifteen—before the paramedics arrived and took over.

James dragged an arm across his forehead, then lurched to his feet, moving out of the way as more equipment was hauled in: stretcher, oxygen tank, defibrillator…

Chaos changed to order as one paramedic issued commands to other members of the first-aid squad.

James circumvented the group to get to Rachel and the man's wife, who was now openly sobbing. An ashen-faced Rachel patted the woman on the shoulder as they both watched the rescue efforts.

"Rachel…"

Both women looked up at him. Rachel's eyes flooded with relief. "James. This is Rosemary."

"Oh, thank you, thank you for helping my poor Henry." The woman grabbed his hands and squeezed them.

"Clear!" a paramedic yelled.

The command echoed through James's head, and he shut out the images of the cardiac unit at Children's Hospital.

Rosemary turned her head toward her husband just as they used the defibrillator on him. She flinched as Henry's body twitched. "Oh! What are they doing to him?"

"They're doing their best to get his heart going again." James draped his arm around her shoulders and gently turned her around. "Why don't we get you a seat over here, out of the way of the traffic?"

"But I want to stay with Henry!"

"You can help the rescue workers the most by staying over here." James assisted the woman to a seat, and a squad member quickly appeared to ask questions about Henry.

"I've got a pulse!" a paramedic proclaimed.

A cheer went up around the restaurant, and Rosemary turned teary eyes at James. She offered him a wavering smile and nodded her head in response to another question from the paramedics.

As the adrenaline rush faded, James's knees turned rubbery, much like the woman's smile. He stumbled to a nearby empty table and sank down into a chair, propping his elbows and covering his face with his hands. He breathed deeply, filling his lungs to capacity; he held the air in for a moment, then exhaled slowly.

It could have been Molly.

He wrestled the thought into submission by reminding himself that despite the fact he had taken the CPR training in case, God forbid, his daughter had needed it, he'd never actually used it before tonight.

Molly was fine, and in the capable—and also CPR-trained—hands of his friends.

Her new heart was healthy and strong.

Everything was fine.

A warm hand closed around his left shoulder, its mate on the right. "She's fine."

"I know. But thanks." He grabbed Rachel's fingers. "How did you know what I was thinking?"

She leaned forward. "I figured there was a reason you knew CPR so well, and I figured you'd be thinking about her, that's all. No psychic powers needed."

James rose from the chair, still clutching her hand. "Good. You're amazing enough without adding special powers to the mix."

He led her back to Rosemary's side. The woman twisted the strap of her purse around her fingers as they loaded her husband onto the gurney. "Do you think he'll be all right?" she asked him.

"The heart is an amazing thing, Rosemary. It's a lot tougher than most of us realize." *Thank God for that.*

They followed the stretcher and paramedics out to the waiting ambulance. One EMT put his hand out when Rosemary tried to climb into the back with her husband. "I'm sorry, ma'am, but we've got two EMTs on board. There's not enough room for you."

"What?" She twisted the bag's handle tighter around her hand. "But...but how am I supposed to get to the hospital? I can't drive now!"

"Rosemary, it's okay." James gently removed the woman's purse from her fingers. He nodded to the paramedic, who slammed the door of the ambulance. Sirens wailing, it charged out of the parking lot. James turned back to the trembling woman. "Where's your car? I'll drive you to the hospital and stay with you until your family arrives, okay?"

Tears filled the woman's eyes. "Bless you! What a darling man you are. The keys are in my bag."

"Good." James turned to Rachel. "You follow us, okay?"

"To...to the h-hospital?"

"That is where they're taking Henry." James accepted the keys from Rosemary. "I'll see you there."

"O-okay, sure."

He knew what it was like to be alone in a hospital while you waited for news from a cardiologist about someone you loved. And he didn't want this woman to go through it that way.

It wasn't until he was driving the old Buick down

the road that he realized Rachel hadn't looked very enthusiastic about the idea. But Rosemary's sobbing didn't leave him time to think about it.

RACHEL'S HEART FELT HEAVY in her chest as she pulled into the parking lot of the county hospital. James, already out of Rosemary's car and standing in the circle of illumination from a streetlight, waved and pointed to the building, then escorted the older woman into the emergency entrance.

Rachel cruised the lot, evaluating and discarding various empty spaces—too close, too far, sandwiched between battered cars, too narrow. If she was lucky, she could play find-a-parking-space until James got Rosemary settled.

But after ten minutes she tired of the game and slipped the convertible into a slot facing the building. Her clammy fingers beat an erratic rhythm on the steering wheel, tempo increasing, then abruptly stopping.

She jumped from the car and slammed the door. Her hands curled into tight fists, fingernails digging into her palms. "You can do this. You ate lasagna tonight. You can do this. Lace those boots tighter and carry on, soldier."

Stiff-legged, she marched through three rows of cars, over the curb and onto the grass, then finally the sidewalk. She paused beneath a droopy maple tree to study the squat, four-story building across the road.

Lights gleamed in various windows—probably patients' rooms. In some of those rooms, people celebrated new life. In others…

Rachel shoved away the thought and the image of Daniel's tiny form in a room similar to those in the building before her. She summoned a picture of James's face instead. He'd called her amazing—and brave.

"Think pleasant thoughts." She started across the road.

Chocolate…James…sex…sex with James and chocolate.

A nervous giggle bubbled out of her. Where had that picture come from?

Better. Definitely better.

She found herself outside the emergency entrance. Squaring her shoulders, she jumped when the automatic doors swung open, then strode through them.

About three steps inside, the scent of antiseptic and cleaning fluids attacked her nose. Her stomach heaved, threatening to return the lasagna. The harsh glare of the fluorescent lights made her blink rapidly.

The nurse at the reception desk scribbled information from a man cradling his towel-wrapped hand in his lap. Murmurs of low voices echoed through the hallway. Rachel swallowed hard and moved toward the waiting area.

Blue plastic chairs—hard-looking, not meant to

be inviting. Small tables cluttered with magazines sporting tattered covers and pamphlets about various diseases. In the corner of the room, a television blared CNN—more crime, more disease, more bad news.

Rachel scanned the small, somber clusters of people, searching for James, but didn't see him.

The automatic doors opened again, and chaos swept into the ER. Several paramedics, voices tense, rushed a gurney down the hallway. "MVA" was one phrase Rachel caught as she pressed against the wall. "Severe head trauma" was another.

Severe head trauma.

The gurney and its cloud of people vanished around the corner. At the far end of the corridor, she saw the form she'd been looking for. James.

Severe head trauma.

A loud roar filled her ears. In her mind, she could hear those same words from a different doctor— *severe head trauma.* And later he'd said "Brain dead."

Her legs trembled as other voices invaded, a stranger, a soft-spoken woman. "We'd like to talk to you about organ donation." Roman: "I think we should, Rachel." Her father: "It makes sense, Rae."

She hadn't wanted it. Couldn't face the thought of them cutting into her baby. She wanted to gather him into her arms despite all the tubes and wires and kiss the boo-boos away. The doctors were wrong. They had to be wrong.

But both her father and Roman thought donation was the right thing to do—that it could save others even though their darling, the light of their lives, was gone.

Daniel.

They'd left her alone with him for a while. She snuggled down next to him on the hard, uncomfortable bed; fixed his ash-blond hair so the bandage on the side of his head wasn't as noticeable, ran her fingertips over his cheeks. He looked so peaceful, her baby, an angel in waiting just like the country music song said. She knew she needed to say goodbye and give him permission to fly.

It had been so hard to get past the fact that—if you didn't count the tubes and such—he looked as if he'd wake up from his nap any minute, throw his arms around her neck and kiss her. Then ask her if she wanted to play cars with him.

Her father's voice had been gruffer than ever before, thick with his own emotion when he'd leaned over the bed and informed her it was time to go.

Daniel. Four-and-a-half years old. Goal in life: to go to kindergarten on the big yellow school bus like the kids his mom taught.

He hadn't made it.

Tears leaked from the corners of her eyes, tears she hadn't dared shed that day in her father's pres-

SUSAN GABLE

ence. They slid down her face, collecting under her chin, on her throat.

Her heart hammered against her breastbone. Her breath came in quick gasps, overloading her with the smells of the hospital despite a rapidly clogging nose: the cleaners, the disinfectants. Death. Blackness obscured the edges of her sight, creating a tunnel-vision effect. Far off in the distance, James turned and looked at her, then he, too, faded into darkness.

"Rachel!" James nearly knocked Don over as he dashed down the corridor. "Rachel!" he repeated, then watched as she slid the rest of the way down the wall and crumpled into a heap at its base.

He dropped to his knees on the hard floor and gathered her into his arms, reassured by the pulse beneath his fingers on her tear-dampened throat. "Rachel? Come on, get back here."

"How much you want to bet this is her first time in a hospital since she lost her son?" Don asked, bending over them both.

"Dammit, I never even thought about that." James slapped her cheeks. "Come on, Rachel. I need smelling salts here!"

"I didn't picture her as a fainter. I thought she was dealing with all of it better than this."

James glared up at him. "She's doing great. Tonight she overcame a conditioned aversion relating to her son's death. Jeez, give her a break. Weren't you the one who told me to stand back and hope she popped? Well, she popped, all right." He turned his attention back to the woman in his arms. "Rachel? Come on, sweetheart, wake up."

A nurse in pink scrubs knelt next to him and waved an ammonia capsule under Rachel's nose.

She inhaled sharply and turned her head away. The persistent nurse followed her with the smelling salts.

Rachel moaned, her eyes fluttering open. Then she began to cough. "No. Get it away."

"Bring that wheelchair over here." An orderly promptly obeyed the nurse, wheeling the chair beside Rachel.

"No. Let me out of here. Gotta get out." Rachel shoved at the nurse's hands.

"Easy, Rachel, everything's all right. Relax and let us get you in this chair. You can lie down for a few minutes and you'll feel much better."

She struggled to sit up. "No. You don't understand. I can't stay here. Not a minute longer." Her hand swung out and gave the wheelchair a shove that sent it wobbling a few feet down the hall. The orderly ambled after it.

Rachel struggled to her feet and made for the doorway.

James sighed and leaned back against the wall. The nurse shook her head and stalked off, no doubt to find a patient who better appreciated her.

Don made a sympathetic clucking sound. He held out a large hand to James. "Let me help you."

"You want to help?" James accepted his hand and rose to his feet.

Don nodded.

"Is your support group over?"

"Yeah, we wrapped about twenty minutes ago."

"Good. Then I need you to stay with Rosemary, the woman we brought to the hospital, until her son gets here. Should be about an hour or so."

"Can do."

James directed Don to Rosemary's location and raced out the ER's automatic doors. He hustled down the sidewalk.

Rachel hadn't gotten far. He found her about fifty feet from the entrance, hugging a streetlight.

"How do you feel?" he asked softly.

"Like I was tap-dancing in combat boots on somebody's damask tablecloth and they yanked it out from under me. Only I didn't stay upright." She clutched the lamppost tighter.

"Still a little dizzy?"

"No, I'm holding this light because it's lonely."

"Oh, really? This is the first time I've seen your sarcastic side." He looped his arm around her waist. "Come on." He led her toward a nearby bench.

"Well get ready, because next you're going to see my *in*side when I throw up my guts along with that lasagna." She moaned as he lowered her to a sitting position and pressed her head forward.

"Put your head between your knees and take deep breaths."

She did as he instructed. He rubbed her back lightly.

After a minute, she looked up at him. "Just please tell me that wasn't Don with you when I came to. Tell me I was hallucinating."

"You want me to lie to you? Why does it matter?"

Her shoulders inched toward her ears, then dropped back down. "I have to sit up." She straightened, running a hand over her hair. The whisper of her sigh floated along the warm breeze.

He waited.

"Take me back to camp, James." She rose from the bench, digging in her pocket. He stood. The keys jingled as she passed them to him. "Let's put the top down and ride with the wind in our hair and pretend we're young and foolish, without a care in the world."

Unshed tears shimmered in her eyes as she lifted her face and offered him an obviously forced smile.

He folded her into his arms and held her tightly, offering comfort. He dropped a kiss on the top of her head, the tangy, lemony scent of her skin and hair stirring feelings of protectiveness in him. "We can do that."

And he could pretend it was all about sex.

And forget the fact that he was starting to really care about this brave and vulnerable woman.

A woman who couldn't set foot in a hospital.

Unlike him and his daughter, who had come to regard Children's Hospital as a second home.

Damn it to hell, why couldn't he pick suitable women?

The wind ruffled his hair as he guided the Goat along the back-country roads. The engine's purr registered only vaguely in his mind. The full moon offered its light from a cloudless sky filled with stars.

Rachel tugged the ponytail holder from her hair, letting it fly free. The blond strands whipped around her face. "That's better."

"Are you ready to talk about what happened in the hospital?"

She turned sideways in the seat as far as her seat belt would allow. Her index and middle fingers pressed gently on his lips. "Not a care in the world, James, remember?"

"And I've told you what happens when you deny and suppress, remember?" He kissed her fingertips to buffer the sting of his words.

"I thought you were my friend?"

"I am your friend. And friends talk about things that trouble them."

"I hate hospitals. I don't want to talk about it."

"But, Rachel—"

She leaned over and cranked on the radio, filling the night air with the loud twang of country music. From the depths of her purse, she pulled out gold-wrapped butterscotch candies, silently offering him one as she popped another into her mouth. He shook his head.

She dropped the candy back into her purse, which she then tucked under the seat. She folded her arms across her chest and turned to look out the side of the car.

The message was loud and clear.

James shifted on the seat, Nolan's plastic "pager" biting into his butt—an unwelcome reminder of where the evening had been headed earlier.

Pretend to be young and foolish, without a care in the world?

He wasn't sure he remembered how.

CHAPTER TWELVE

"WHAT-IF" WASN'T A GAME Rachel liked to play. It hurt too much. But tonight, if James hadn't been there with his CPR skills, a man might have died.

The radio and the Goat's engine fell silent as James shut off the ignition. He removed the keys and held them out to her. "Thanks for letting me drive."

"I wasn't in any shape, and we both know it."

"You let me drive to the restaurant, too."

She shrugged. "I thought you'd enjoy it." Bending down, she retrieved her purse from beneath the seat, then climbed from the car. Wordlessly, they worked together to put the convertible's top up.

James circled around the car to her side. "Rachel, I'm sorry things didn't go better. Not exactly what I had in mind for our date."

"Me, neither." She tipped her head back and looked up at him. "But the night's not over yet. I was thinking about taking a walk down by the lake. Would you like to come?"

His fingers brushed over her hair. "Yes, I would."

"Okay. Just let me get some things." She opened

the trunk. An old comforter—one she and Daniel had often used for picnics—and a flashlight lay in the corner. Rachel pulled them out, clicking the light on. "I found a wonderful place. Follow me, but watch your step. There are a lot of rocks and roots in the path."

The moon added its glow, filtering down through the gently swaying trees. Weeds and tall grass covered what had once been a viable path; low shrubs encroached along the edges. Rachel picked her way along the route.

It led to a small, manmade beach along a secluded cove, tucked away from the main part of the lake. Rachel loved the spot and had come here several times. "Here we are." She spread out the comforter on the sand, then sank down on it. "What do you think?"

James lowered himself beside her. "How did you find this? It's great."

"On one of my early-morning walks." She tipped her head back. "Just look at all those stars."

James shifted until he sat behind her, his legs surrounding hers, arms enfolding her waist. "How's that?"

With a contented sigh, she relaxed, molding her body against his, allowing her head to rest against his shoulder. "It's nice," she murmured. "Very nice."

"Mmm, I think so, too."

The companionable silence was broken only by

the occasional throaty love song of a frog and the ripples of the nearby water. A balmy breeze gently fanned her loose hair. Rachel snuggled deeper into the warmth of the man who held her so tenderly.

Fireflies flickered in the shrubs and grasses surrounding their private spot. "Molly would have a field day with all these fireflies," she said.

"Probably." James nuzzled her hair.

"They're like echoes of the stars." Rachel tipped her head again and studied the heavens. "Doesn't nature make you feel small and insignificant?"

"Small and insignificant? Not really. Awestruck at the vastness of it all, maybe. Is that the same as feeling small?"

She said nothing for several moments as the lake lapped gently along the shore.

"I realized something tonight," she said finally.

"What's that?"

"Life's short. It's just a blip in the grand scheme of things." Her hand swept across the air. "Just a blip. I realized that if there are things you want in life, you shouldn't put them off, you should go ahead and do them. I mean, Daniel," she sighed, "Daniel wanted to get on a big yellow school bus and go to kindergarten. There's no way I could have speeded that up for him. But take Henry and Rosemary. Maybe they've always wanted to go to Europe but kept putting it off. Tonight, they almost ran out of chances."

He cupped her face with his hand, thumb lightly

caressing her cheekbone. "And what is it you want before you run out of chances, sweet Rachel?"

Heat rose beneath the skin he stroked, spreading across her face and down her body. She swallowed hard, then took the plunge. "You," she whispered. "I want you."

His thumb stilled on her face. He closed his eyes. "Rachel, I..."

A sharp pain radiated across her chest, into her stomach. Had she misread him earlier? "Don't you feel the same way?"

His eyes flashed open. "I want you, Rachel. It's just..."

"What?"

"I can't promise you a future, and you deserve someone who can give you that kind of security."

Her heart warmed and softened, a marshmallow over an open flame. "Oh, James. That's the first time anyone has put my needs first."

"And I mean it." He dipped his head, barely brushing his lips over hers.

She closed her eyes and angled her head, waiting to feel his mouth on hers.

Suddenly his hand left her face. Startled, she opened her eyes to see him jump to his feet.

"James, wait!" She leapt up as well. "Don't go."

"Rachel, I'm sorry. But if I stay here, I'm going to do something you might regret in the morning."

"Something like make love to me? Like I want

you to?'' She didn't wait for his answer. Life was too short, and James was a very special man. She stepped close to him and flattened her palms against his chest. ''I'm not asking for forever, James. I'm not even asking for tomorrow. I'm interested in right now, tonight. This moment may well be all we ever have, but I'm not willing to let it go by.'' She slipped her hands between his elbows and torso, wrapping her arms around his waist. ''Are you?''

He didn't move.

She let her fingers explore the broad planes of his back. Could she seduce him? That was something else she'd never done. Throwing caution into the lake, she trailed her right hand lower, caressed the firm curve of his behind.

James inhaled sharply. His hips moved forward, pressing his erection against her belly. ''Rachel...''

She lifted her fingers to his lips, lightly traced their outline. ''Your mouth says no, but your body says yes.'' She slipped her arm from around his waist and stepped back. ''But, if you really don't want to...''

She crossed to the center of the comforter, kicking off her sandals. Her fingers opened the top two buttons of her blouse.

''W-what are you doing?''

''Well, I've never gone skinny-dipping. And I think that's one of those things that should definitely be experienced in life, don't you?'' Her fingers continued to work on the row of buttons as she talked.

The moonlight caressed her bare shoulders as she slowly lowered the garment. James wanted to be that moonbeam, sliding across her satiny skin. A lacy bra cupped her small breasts. She tossed the blouse to the edge of the comforter and lowered her hand to the button on her capris.

He had to remind himself to breathe.

The rasp of the zipper teeth echoed loudly in the little cove. She shimmied the tight denim over her hips, turning around to give him a full view of that perfect backside as the pants dropped to her feet.

''Oh, God.'' A thong. The woman actually wore a tiny, sexy, satin thong. ''Rachel.'' He barely recognized his own voice, it was so raspy and thick.

She turned back to face him, a vision in moonlight and skimpy lingerie. ''Something wrong?''

''Yeah. You take my breath away.''

She dipped her head, a shy smile on her lips.

Two quick strides brought him to her. He cradled her face in his hands. ''You're absolutely sure about this?''

She nodded.

He lowered his head and kissed her. Hard. Sweet butterscotch, warm woman... He slid his hands around her back, trailing down her smooth skin. The strings of her thong guided him lower, and he lightly ran his fingers over her curves. He tucked his hands around the silken flesh, pulled her against him.

Her tiny shudder and moan deepened his desire. He trailed kisses down her neck, lingering in the hollow of her throat.

Her hands pulled frantically at his shirt. "I want to feel you against me."

He yanked it over his head and dropped it to the ground. "This, too," he said, reaching behind her to struggle with the clasp of her bra. His out-of-practice fingers fumbled until the fabric gave way. He slid the straps down her arms and tossed the garment aside, too.

She pressed against him, the hard tips of her breasts igniting flames of desire.

He scooped her up and placed her on the blanket, propping himself on his elbow over her.

She folded her arms over her chest, a flicker of apprehension in her eyes.

"Don't cover them, Rachel." He gently moved her arms, watching her face carefully. "I want to look at you."

She pressed her lips tightly together. "They're…"

"Beautiful," he pronounced. With one fingertip, he teased the nipple to attention.

"Small." She gasped as he cupped her breast in his palm.

"Perfect. Good things come in small packages."

"I'd like to know your reaction if I say that when you drop your pants."

Laughter erupted from deep in his belly. "Aah, Rachel. You *do* make me feel young and foolish, like I haven't a care in the world." He leaned over to nibble on her earlobe, then whispered, "But I don't think I'll disappoint you."

She smiled and caressed him through his jeans. "Me, neither."

He groaned and grabbed her wrist in a viselike grip. "Honey, I've ached all night over you. It's been such a long time for me, and all I want to do is bury myself deep inside you. You touch me like that and the fireworks will be over before we even get started."

She flexed her fingers, teasing him with a light touch even while he still held her hand. "Really?"

His turn to gasp. "Really. Wicked...sexy... woman."

"Only with you," she whispered. "You make me feel that way."

"Your husband was an idiot."

She giggled and stroked him again.

He lowered his head and hesitated, his warm mouth poised just over her breast, just out of reach, teasing, tormenting. "Two can play like that." He circled her nipple with the tip of his tongue, making her moan. "Why don't you tell me the pleasurable image you pictured back in the restaurant? The one that made you flush so nicely and catch your breath?''

She ran her fingers through his hair. ''Oh, uh, you're on the right…right track.''

He lifted his head and grinned at her. ''Really? Let me see if I can follow the track correctly.'' He showered her body with kisses, starting between her breasts and trailing lower. She sucked in her breath when he kissed her navel, then circled it with his tongue, but stopped breathing completely when he probed just under the elastic of her thong. ''Don't hold your breath, Rachel. I don't want you fainting again. It's tough on the male ego during sex—unless you wait until your climax. Then, by all means, go ahead.'' He winked. Grinning up at her from between her thighs, he placed his mouth gingerly on her panties.

Rachel felt scorching heat rocket through her. ''You—you don't have to…''

''No, I don't have to. I want to. Lift up.''

She raised her hips and he peeled the thong from her body.

She clutched at the comforter when he began to lavish the attention of his mouth on her. Nimble fingers joined the game, leaving her panting when they teased and retreated.

She scrunched her eyes shut. He increased the pace of his actions until she finally exploded. ''James!'' She rode the strong climax that washed over her.

Eventually, she opened her eyes to find him blocking her view of the sky, a Cheshire cat grin on his face. "Pleasurable stimulus?"

She nodded, unable to speak.

"Good. Now that we've had the appetizer, how about the main course?" He pressed his lower body against hers, and she realized that he'd shed his pants. And shorts.

His naked arousal skimmed the juncture of her thighs, and panic overwhelmed her. "Wait! James, wait." She shoved against his chest. "We can't. Not without—"

"Easy, sweetheart. I know." He reached to the side and held up a packet. "Not without this. Guaranteed fresh, okay? It hasn't been on the shelf forever."

Tears filled her eyes and she blinked them back. His consideration knew no bounds. How many men would remember her concern? She smiled, hoping her lips didn't quiver. "Thank you."

He caressed her body with his fingers and mouth, increasing her desire again. "Ready?" he murmured against her neck.

"Oh, yes. I want you inside me."

He rolled away for only a moment, preparing himself, then he hovered over her. "Rachel, this might be a little fast, if so—"

"Shh. Don't talk!" Hands around his bottom, she urged him forward.

In one easy motion, he was inside her.

"Oh, sweet Rachel."

She felt him struggle for control. He slid out, starting a slow tempo. His fingers slipped between their sweat-slicked bodies to caress her where they joined.

"Oh, James!"

"That's it, Rachel. Come with me."

As she let herself go, Rachel felt James launch himself with her. His elbow trembled with the exertion of holding himself over her. He kissed her thoroughly, then dropped down beside her, rolled onto his back, and gathered her into his arms.

Their ragged breathing slowly evened out, and the roaring in her ears gave way to the sounds of the night: the wind in the trees and the frog chorus. James tugged the edges of the comforter around them and nuzzled the top of her head. "That was incredible."

"Mmm." Her fingers traced lazy spirals on his stomach. "It sure was."

Her naked body pressed against his, combined with the lemony scent of her skin, the fresh air. In the stillness he could hear the murmur of a nearby brook feeding into the lake. Blessed relaxation stole through his body, loosening every muscle, dissolving all the tension. "This beats a hammock any day," he murmured.

"A hammock? You've done it in a hammock?"

He chuckled. "No, I mean for relaxing. I don't think I've felt this good in…maybe never."

"I'm glad."

The comfortable silence enveloped them again. He kept stroking her hair. Though sated physically, he craved more. They'd been intimate, he'd been inside her body—and now he wanted to know everything about her. He longed to ask her about her son.

But he didn't want to spoil the moment.

For either of them.

"James?"

"Mmm?"

"Tell me about Molly's heart."

The muscles behind his neck knotted. Apparently they'd been thinking along the same lines. "Molly's heart? What brought that up? I thought we were young and foolish, without a care in the world right now?"

"Sorry." She shifted her head. "It's just that I'm lying here, listening to your strong, steady heartbeat, and thinking about Molly and how amazing she is."

He smiled in the darkness. "She is. What is it you want to know?"

"What…what kind of a prognosis does she have? Do you know anything about her donor?"

"Her prognosis is pretty good. They can't give me a definitive answer on how long she will live because the truth is, transplant medicine is still kind of a new frontier."

"I guess none of us knows how long we—or our children—have."

Pain laced her voice, and he tightened his arms around her. "That's very true."

"What about her donor's family? Did you ever get in touch with them?"

"I sent a thank-you card. Hardest thing I ever wrote. Every time I reread it, it sounded so lame. Words can't express how grateful I am to them for saving my little girl's life or how sorry I am about their little girl. They didn't write back, though."

"I—" her voice caught "—I can understand that."

"I'm sure you can." He stroked up and down her back.

"I got some stuff from the Organ Procurement Organization, including a letter about two weeks after... I didn't even open it."

"Not ready?" he asked gently.

"No, not ready. And believe me, I tried a few times. But maybe when I go home, I'll dig it out."

Pride in her progress welled inside him. "Will you tell me more about Daniel?"

"Like what?"

"Like, what was his favorite color? TV show? Did he sleep with a night-light or was he a tough guy?"

Voice soft, she talked about her son, his love for yellow and vehicles of all shapes and sizes, his teddy bear, and his night-light. "He always had a smile for everyone."

"He must have taken after his mom," he said.

"Hmm. You know, I used to worry that he'd grow up and take after his father...."

He cuddled her closer. "With you for a mom, I doubt that would have happened. He would have grown up knowing how to appreciate a woman, and looking far and wide for one who could measure up to you."

A blur of white streaked across the night sky, and Rachel tensed at the same time he did. Grateful for the distraction, he nudged her shoulder. "A shooting star!" It faded as quickly as it had flared into life.

"I saw it."

"Did you make a wish?"

"Now I know you meant it when you said you were a wish-believer. Which do you think is more powerful, a wish on a shooting star, or a firefly wish?"

He rolled over, positioning them both on their sides, face-to-face. He reached out to stroke her cheek. "Well, I don't know. My firefly wish for a kiss sure came true in a really big way." Leaning forward, he brushed his mouth over hers—tentatively at first, then he deepened it, pressing more firmly, coaxing her with the tip of his tongue until she opened to him.

Several minutes later, he surfaced for air. "I've got another wish. Want to hear it?"

Her eyes fluttered open, dreamy desire evident in them. She nodded.

"I wish to make love to you again."

She pressed her belly harder against his erection. "Tell me something I don't know." She smiled at him.

"Okay, did you know that this time, I'd like to do it in a bed?" He groaned and reached beneath his side. "I think I'm lying on a rock."

She chuckled. "All right. My place or yours?"

"Yours is closer." He kissed the tip of her nose. "I'll race you there."

"Race? Aren't you worried we'll fall and get hurt?"

He threw the comforter off them and reached for his clothes. "I'm more worried we won't make it there fast enough, and I'll end up grabbing you and making love to you in front of the cabins."

"Good thing I'm at the end of the line, then."

"But that won't save us from the rocks." Shirt still hanging open, feet shoved into shoes without socks, he gathered up the blanket. "Don't button too many," he warned Rachel as she fumbled with her blouse.

A slow grin curved her mouth. "Don't want to work too hard when we get there, huh?"

"You got it."

She flicked on the flashlight. "Let's go."

Just one night, he reminded himself as he followed her along the path. One incredible night, a night he'd never forget.

But as he watched her hurry ahead of him, he wondered if one night would be enough. If one week would be enough.

In her arms, he remembered what it was to be just a man.

His thoughts turned to his daughter. Molly didn't deserve to be relegated to second place. It wasn't her fault she needed so much of his time. And he wouldn't change her for anything. He loved her exactly the way she was.

His pace slowed, and the gap between Rachel and him lengthened. Amazing how much clearer he could think when she wasn't close.

When he walked up the creaky steps and onto her porch, she was already waiting, cabin door open. He followed her inside and dumped the comforter onto a chair.

She propped one hip against the back of the sofa, angled her head and studied him for a moment. "Our night's over already, huh?"

Disappointment was evident in her blue eyes. He shook his head. "Not over. Just temporarily interrupted. I need to check on her."

"I understand."

"I figured you would." He strode to the cabin phone, then checked the time. Only 10:42. Nolan would still be awake; he was a notorious night owl.

"I'll just freshen up while you make your call," Rachel said, heading for the bathroom.

He waved her off. The phone rang only once, then Nolan's voice came across the line. "Hello?"

"Hey. It's me."

"Who else would it be? She's fine. I dragged her and Cherish into the cabin about thirty minutes ago, and they're settled in for the night. Go make use of those things I gave you and stop worrying."

"Worrying comes naturally. Are you sure she's okay?"

"Listen, she's tucked into bed, snug as a bug in a rug. They're both probably sound asleep by now." A raucous burst of little girl shrieks from the background nixed that idea.

"What's going on? Should I come down and get her?"

Pattering feet, and murmurs about shadows and monkey paws and something he didn't catch crept across the phone lines. Giggles followed, reassuring him.

"No, it's just these two are determined to keep me from my date with my wife."

"Hey, bud, it's only one night." James laughed.

"I have no desire to follow in your chaste footsteps. Now, hang up and turn your attention back to that pretty lady you're with. You are still with her, right?"

He glanced at the closed bathroom door. The sound of running water came from the other side.

He grinned as an image of the two of them, beneath the spray of the shower, skin slicked with soap came to his mind.

"Still with her. Tell Molly I love her."

"Will do. 'Night, Jim."

Father responsibilities complete, James hung up and turned his attention back to the bathroom door. He shed his shirt, draping it over the coffee table. Friday night was still young—and for this night, so was he. Young, foolish, and with his cares tucked safely in bed, in the capable hands of his friends.

He pushed the bathroom door open a crack. Steam rushed out. "Rachel? You up for some company in there?"

Water streamed down her face as she peeked around the rainbow-covered shower curtain. "I thought you'd never ask." She chuckled. "I thought you might find this a better idea than skinny-dipping in the lake. Fewer germs."

"Hmm, you may be right about that. Maybe I should climb in there and make sure you don't miss any. Full body search for germs."

She crooked a finger at him. "So what are you waiting for? Lose those pants and come on in."

He eagerly accepted her invitation.

CHAPTER THIRTEEN

THE MAN DRIVING THE SUV while Rachel sat in the passenger's seat was very different from the one who'd slipped into the shower with her a mere twenty-four hours earlier. That man had embraced the young-and-foolish credo of the night; this one was...she searched for the right word. *Brooding*. This version of James was definitely brooding.

They'd spent Saturday at a little amusement park in Erie. Camp Firefly Wishes had provided free passes, along with bus transportation to those who needed it. Rachel had planned on a quiet day at camp with all the families gone, but to her surprise and Molly's delight, James had invited her to tag along with them.

And now he obviously regretted that decision. She shifted on her seat, angling to face him. She spoke softly in deference to the little girl sleeping in the back seat. "You're mad at me."

"I'm not mad."

She studied his profile in the green illumination from the dash. "You seem mad."

"Well, I'm not."

"Excuse me, Dr. McClain, but didn't you tell me

that not expressing your emotions was a bad thing?''

''I'm not *mad,* Rachel. I'm just…''

''What?''

He exhaled loudly. ''Slightly annoyed. You undercut my authority as a parent today.''

She wanted to touch him, to lay her hand against his arm and communicate her discontent. But she didn't dare, not while he was driving. ''I didn't mean to. I'm sorry, James. I had no idea you wouldn't want her on that roller coaster. For crying out loud, it's just one step above a kiddie coaster. In fact…'' She trailed off, not wanting to explain how much Daniel had wanted to ride that particular coaster during their last outing to Waldameer, and she'd promised him that the next year, he could. That he'd be big enough then.

Taking Molly on the Comet while her dad had been off to the rest rooms hadn't been an act of subversion on Rachel's part, it had been an act of remembrance. The little girl had been so excited by the prospect, Rachel got swept along with her enthusiasm. And Molly had loved it. At least until they'd gotten off the ride and come face-to-face with a very unhappy James.

''What?'' he asked.

''Nothing. I'm sorry. I didn't mean to go around you. But Molly obviously survived the ride—in fact, she had a good time. You keep her on such a short leash. No swimming, no bumper cars, no roller coasters…when Cherish, who has the same condition, does all those things and more. I thought you said you brought her to camp to have a normal summer and some fun?''

''She's having fun.''

The hum of the SUV's air-conditioning filled the hole in the conversation as Rachel decided the point wasn't worth arguing. She was trying to make up with the man, not antagonize him. She watched out the window as the dark shapes of trees darted past.

A low moan emerged from the back seat. James cast a quick glance over his shoulder. ''Molly? Honey, are you all right?''

''No-o-o.''

''What's wrong?''

''I think I'm gonna barf. Pull over. Now!''

As the car came to a stop, Rachel vaulted out onto the side of the road. Molly'd already popped open her door and bolted for the grass. Rachel held the long red ponytail with one hand and rubbed Molly's back with the other while the poor kid threw up. Gravel scuffed as James crossed behind the vehicle and joined them.

When Molly finally straightened, Rachel went to the car and returned with several napkins—she'd known James would have a supply in the glove box—and a bottle of water. ''Here, honey, swish your mouth out with this.''

''I hope you don't have food poisoning from something you ate.''

Molly wiped her face with the tissue. "More like everything I ate," she mumbled. "Oh, Dad, you're right. Too much junk food is bad for you."

"Too much junk food?" James guided his daughter back into the SUV.

Rachel climbed into the passenger's seat and turned around to see Molly nod glumly. "I was sneaking food all day. I had funnel cake, and cotton candy, lemonade, ice cream, fudge, French fries, part of a candy apple and a chocolate chip cookie." She sighed and slumped against the beige leather as he fastened her seat belt without a word, slammed the door and climbed back in the front.

He glared at Rachel before starting the engine and turning off the flashers.

She held her hands up. "Don't look at me. I swear, I did not sneak your child treats behind your back."

Molly moaned softly as the car pulled onto the highway. "Don't blame Miss Rachel, Dad. She didn't know I was helping myself to her snacks, and Cherish's and Nolan's. She was too busy looking at you when you weren't looking."

Heat rose in Rachel's cheeks. She adjusted the air-conditioning vents, aiming them onto her face.

James cleared his throat. "Let this be a lesson to you, young lady. I don't say no just because I like to hear myself say it."

Molly mumbled her less-than-enthusiastic agreement.

The rest of the ride to camp passed uneventfully. When they parked in front of the little blue cabin, Rachel gathered up her purse and slid from the SUV. James met her at the car door.

"Thanks for inviting me. I had a good time," she said. "Well, mostly."

"I'd like to make up for that 'mostly' part. You want to hang around a few minutes while I get Molly settled in bed?"

"Okay. Should I wait out here?"

"Wherever. In the living room, on the porch, just make yourself comfortable." James opened the back door and unfastened Molly's seat belt, then scooped the sleeping child into his arms. Her head lolled against his shoulder, and for a moment, Rachel didn't know which of them she envied more—the child or the parent. Many times she'd carried Daniel in a similar fashion. She walked ahead of James and held the screened door open, then ducked around him to open the cabin's main door.

"Thanks," he murmured. "I'll be right back."

James wrestled with his emotions as he carted Molly to her bedroom. He was mad at himself for being petty with Rachel. He knew she hadn't undercut him intentionally. He'd mentally kicked himself the moment he'd seen the excitement leave both her and Molly's faces when he'd confronted them after the roller coaster. But still…he had his rules, and Molly had to live by them.

He laid his daughter on the far side of the double

bed, then took off her sneakers and socks. She hated sleeping with a ponytail—always complained the next morning how much it hurt. So James carefully worked the rubber band out and freed the thick, shoulder-length waves. He pulled back the covers, then tucked her in, clothes and all. She stirred slightly. "Don't forget…kiss me good-night."

"Never happen, Unsinkable." He brushed a strand of hair from her forehead as she groaned at the nickname, then pressed his lips against the same spot. The skin temperature was cool, so he decided the upset stomach was probably from all the junk food. "I love you."

"Love you, too. Don't forget to kiss Miss Rachel good-night, too."

The idea held great appeal. There had been moments at the park when he'd had to fight the urge to take Rachel's hand in his. And having her lean against him, cradled between his spread thighs while they rode the log flume, had been utter torture. Delightful torture, but torture nonetheless. It provoked too many images of last night's lovemaking. "Hey. We agreed that kissing is totally my business, not yours."

"Mmm-hmm." Molly rolled over onto her side and snuggled into the pillow and covers as James flicked the switch and pulled the door partially closed.

The only light in the main room came from the one over the kitchen sink and the porch, so he waited a moment for his eyes to adjust. Rachel stood just inside the cottage, near the table. "Come and sit with me for a few minutes." He gestured toward the sofa. "I want to explain my behavior today."

"You don't have to explain."

"I don't have to, but I want to. Need to." He waved at the couch again. "Come on. Please?"

"All right."

She sat at one end and he in the middle. He turned sideways to face her, his arm draped along the back of the couch. "I know you didn't mean to undermine my authority today. I'm sorry I even said that. It's just…well, for one thing, I'm not used to having anyone else make decisions where Molly's concerned."

Rachel gave him a weak smile. "If I were writing your report card, I'd have to put 'Doesn't share well with others,' huh?"

"I guess." He shrugged. "She's my life, Rachel. After being around all these other transplant parents for a week, I'm starting to see that maybe I'm a bit overprotective—"

"A bit?" Her smile widened.

"All right, maybe a *little* more than a bit. But I almost lost her. And the idea of that, it…scares the hell out of me."

Compassion flooded her eyes. "I can understand that."

"So I'm forgiven?" He brushed his fingertips over her shoulder.

"There's nothing to forgive. You're a concerned dad, that's all."

Looking at the soft features of her face, letting his fingers dance over the smooth skin at the back of her neck, being a concerned dad was rapidly fading from his mind. "I've waited all day for this," he whispered, leaning forward and pressing his mouth to hers for a brief kiss.

"What about Molly?" Rachel splayed her hands across his chest and pushed him back a fraction of an inch.

"She's sleeping." He caressed the line of her jaw. "So, what were you thinking about when you were stealing looks at me today?"

"Last night." A flush appeared in her cheeks and she averted her eyes.

James held back a groan as a rush of heat raced through his veins. "Last night was…great."

She hesitantly met his gaze again. "For me, too."

"Look, Rachel, I don't know if we'll get the chance to be…*that* intimate again, not with Molly around. But I don't want to waste a second of the time we can steal together."

The lines around her mouth softened and she smiled. "Then I suggest, counselor, that you shut up and kiss me."

He pulled her against his chest and did as she

commanded, loving the way she made him feel. Carefree, alive, very much a man...

One more week with her was not going to be enough.

"COME ON IN." DON SWUNG the door to his office wide and offered a sweep of his arm in invitation.

Rachel surreptitiously wiped her palms across the hem of her T-shirt as she entered. Don's office was larger than Trudy's, featuring more than just the standard desk and filing cabinets. A sofa and armchair occupied one corner, and there was a large table with four hard-backed chairs around it in another. And he had an air conditioner, for which she was very grateful. Maybe her hands would stop sweating.

Don dropped himself into the armchair, leaving her no option but to sit on the couch.

Hard to believe two weeks had passed since she'd arrived. The hours she'd spent with James had made time fly. Early-morning walks with him and Molly, evenings spent around the campfire behind his cabin. An occasional touch, a few stolen kisses. Though they hadn't made love again, Rachel treasured what they'd shared.

"So, Rachel, tell me, has Camp Firefly Wishes done anything for you?"

Okay, this was it. Her last chance to influence the report Don would undoubtedly be writing in the next few days. She nodded her head. "I think so."

"What?"

"Well, meeting these kids has made me—" the next words caught in her throat and she had to force them out "—glad that I agreed to donate Daniel's organs."

Don scribbled on the legal-size yellow tablet he'd propped on the arm of the chair. "What else?"

She lifted both shoulders. "I don't know. It's reminded me that life is for living, and I should get on with doing that. No matter how hard it is."

"Good."

They talked about the kids in her care, and the responses of the parents to her, about her performance as the arts and crafts teacher. Don skirted around the issue of her relationship with James and Molly. The camp director must have noticed something going on between them, but Rachel appreciated the fact that he didn't seem interested in discussing it.

"Let's talk about the night in the hospital."

All the moisture from her mouth fled to her hands, causing a new round of sweating. She picked at a seam on the sofa's cushion. "I'd rather not."

"I'd like to know what you were thinking, what you were feeling that led up to your collapse, Rachel." Don's pen poised over the pad.

In an instant, she could smell the disinfectants, hear the sounds of the sirens and the babble of nurses, see Daniel in that bed, all hooked up to monitors. "No!" She surged to her feet. "I am not talking about that, I am *not* thinking about that!"

"Easy. We're just talking here. Talking can't hurt you." Don rose, hand outstretched.

"No. I'm leaving. Enough is enough. You'll have to write your report however you see fit, but I'm not talking about this with you. Or anyone else!" She rushed out the door, the muggy air in the hallway making it hard to breathe.

Her first impulse was to run to James. In his company she could forget about the bad stuff, the painful stuff. But what was the point in that? Tomorrow they were both leaving camp, he to Branford Fields, in the southwest corner of Pennsylvania, she to Elsworth, in the northwest corner. And that would be the end of it. Now was the time to stand on her own two feet. She pinched the bridge of her nose, hard.

Sometimes life was a bitch.

But a good soldier laced her boots tighter and carried on.

JAMES STEPPED NEARER to Rachel in the shadows on the edge of the beach. The camp's closing ceremony was just about over, and so was their time together.

And he didn't like that idea one bit.

"And so, we extinguish the memory torch until next year, but we'll carry in our hearts the memories of the people we've loved and lost, and the memories of the people who made such a difference for others, giving life in a time of loss.'' Don's solemn voice echoed over the crowd as he snuffed out the flame atop the rainbow-colored torch. Black smoke drifted upward in the night sky. ''We hope to see a lot of you again next year. May you all be happy and healthy between now and then.''

James captured Rachel's hand as it headed for her face. He wove their fingers together and squeezed, knowing Don's words had stirred memories of her little boy.

''Darn! I can't believe camp is over already,'' Molly complained from his other side. ''Now we gotta go back home, and the rest of the summer is going to be boring. I wanna stay longer.''

So did James. He wasn't ready to give up on Rachel, on feeling like a more complete human being than he had in ages. Their stolen moments over the past week had been welcome oases in his life. She'd pushed him to try things with Molly. A trail ride on horseback, a canoe trip on the lake…but it was some of the other times he'd miss more. Her watching him tuck Molly in at night, his pulling her onto the porch where they'd talked and kissed like a couple of teenagers. But all that was over. He stifled the urge to sigh. ''Sorry, tiger. That's the way it goes. Before you know it, school will be back in session.''

''Oh, great. I can hardly wait.''

Rachel chuckled.

The crowd slowly dispersed, making its way off the beach, wandering back in the direction of the individual cabins. Nolan, Michelle and Cherish appeared in the throng. Nolan carried Tyler in an infant seat, but used his free hand to clap James on the shoulder. ''Well, Jim, I guess that's about it for our vacations, huh? Back to work on Monday. How about one last campfire at your place?''

''Please, Dad, please?'' Molly clasped her hands together in supplication. ''Just one more night? We can catch some more fireflies, and tell more stories.''

''Roast a few more marshmallows,'' Cherish put in. ''After tonight, I won't get to see Molly again for a long time. Please?''

James pretended to consider it for a moment, when the truth was, he was as eager as they were to prolong the experience. ''Okay.''

The girls shrieked and jumped up and down. ''We'll meet you there!'' Molly grabbed Cherish by the hand and the pair took off down the road, weaving around other groups of campers.

''You'll join us, right?'' he asked Rachel.

''Huh?'' She looked up from the dirt road to his face. ''Join you for what?''

''A campfire. Behind my cabin. Roasted marshmallows and stories.'' James waved off Nolan and Michelle, who picked up their pace, leaving him alone with Rachel.

''I should pack. I planned an early start tomorrow

morning.'' Right. Like she was really looking forward to getting back home to her empty house…her empty life. Even her cat wouldn't be glad to see her—Peggy Sue was probably miffed at being left with Mrs. Benton for so long. And what would Rachel do for the next few weeks, until it was time to get ready for school? Sit around and watch the paint peel?

Jolted, she realized that was exactly what she had been doing since Daniel had died. Zoning out. Avoiding everyone and anyone.

''Rachel?'' James tightened his fingers around hers. ''You okay?'' he asked softly.

''I'm fine.''

He bobbed his head. ''Of course. What other answer did I expect? How about you pack first, then come to the fire?''

She stopped as they reached the front of his cabin and turned to face him. ''I wouldn't miss it for anything.'' *Just like I wouldn't have missed these two weeks with you, James McClain.*

''Good. Then I'll see you in a little while.''

''So, James, was summer camp all you'd hoped for?'' Michelle shifted from foot to foot as she rocked the baby in her arms, the glow from the fire casting flickering shadows across her face.

Nolan had taken the girls off to catch fireflies one last time. The wind rustled the tops of the trees and swirled the smoke from the fire, lifting tiny red embers into the air.

"All that and more." He smiled. Let Michelle make of that what she wanted.

"So I noticed. There's been a certain spring in your step the past week." She settled the now-sleeping infant into his carrying seat, then tucked a lightweight blanket around him. "I hate to admit it, but it looks good on you."

"What looks good on me?" He glanced down at the shirt he wore, a yellow-colored polo.

"Not your shirt, nitwit. Rachel."

"Rachel?" He raised his eyebrows as Michelle sank into the lawn chair. "I thought you didn't approve of me and Rachel? She has too much baggage, I believe you said. Or is it that you can approve now that camp's just about over?"

"I worried, and I shouldn't have. She's been really good with the kids." Michelle cocked her head as Nolan's booming laughter echoed from the front of the cabin. She broke into an easy grin. "It's not good to be alone, James. I was concerned about the effects Rachel's…loss…could have on you and Molly. I was wrong."

James slapped his hand across his chest. "Write this down in the record books. Michelle was wrong."

"Smart-ass. So, you gonna keep seeing her? I checked out a map on the Internet yesterday and Branford Fields is only about a two-hour drive or so from Elsworth. Weekends would be easily do-able.''

Weekends. With Rachel. The thought appealed to him. And he'd already checked out the distance be-tween their respective small towns. Definitely do-able. ''I don't know, Michelle. What if Molly starts to read too much into the relationship? I'd hate to see her get hurt.''

Or Rachel. The memory of her collapsing in the hospital flashed by. *Or me.*

Michelle sighed and shook her head. ''You can't protect her from everything. Besides, you ought to know by now exactly how resilient the human heart is.''

James leaned back in the chair, stretching his legs out and crossing them at the ankles. He laced his fingers together and cupped his head in his palms. Crickets chirped, competing with the occasional throaty croak of a frog along the lake's edge. The wood smoke smelled pleasant. ''I don't even know if she'd want to keep seeing me, Michelle. For all I know, she's fine with the whole summer romance thing we originally agreed to.''

''You'll never know if you don't ask. For once in your life, take a risk, James.'' The sound of little-girl giggles drifted around the cabin, followed by Nolan's mock roar, and then, high-pitched shrieks. Michelle laughed. ''Maybe you'll get as lucky as I did.''

A few trial weekends. He and Molly could visit

Rachel's house; she could stay with them. In the guest room. He wouldn't give the wrong impression to Molly—even if they were sleeping together, they weren't going to be "sleeping together."

He leapt from the chair and bolted in the direction of Rachel's cabin, hoping to catch her before she even finished packing. And hoping she'd agree to keep seeing him. "Be right back! Keep an eye on Molly for me!"

"James!" Michelle yelled after him. "Don't run in the dark. You'll fall!"

Quite possibly.

And the thought didn't scare him as much as he'd expected.

He slowed to a trot outside her cabin, vaulted up the steps and onto her porch. He rapped on the door, then opened it. "Rachel?"

"In the bedroom. Come on in, James."

He found her packing—again, though this time she was more organized. Her dresser didn't look as if it had exploded. She turned from placing something into her suitcase and offered him a slight smile. "Did you bring me more fireflies?"

He shook his head. "No. But I brought you something else."

"Oh?"

He crooked his finger at her from the doorway. "Come over here."

When she was close enough, he reached out and pulled her into his arms. She tipped her head, looking up at him. Closing the space between them slowly, he leaned forward and eased his lips against hers. For several minutes they kissed, her hands fastened tightly on the points of his collar as she held him near. Finally he rested his forehead against hers. "Ah, sweet Rachel. Any regrets?"

"No," she said softly. "Well, just one." She smiled at him.

"What's that?"

"I wish we'd had another chance—" she broke eye contact and her cheeks flushed "—to make love."

He ran his fingers along her back. "So do I. Maybe we can do something about it."

"Isn't everyone waiting at the campfire?"

"I'm not talking about right now." He lifted his head from hers and took her hands in his. "Rachel, two weeks isn't enough. I want more than this. I was hoping you'd agree to see me on weekends in the future."

"Weekends?"

"Yep. We could take turns. One weekend you come to my place, one weekend Molly and I come to yours." He searched her eyes for a hint of reaction as she stared at him. "Well?"

A broad smile broke across her face and she nodded. "I think that sounds like a fantastic idea." Her fingers tightened around his.

"Great," he said, lowering his mouth toward hers again. "Then tonight isn't goodbye. It's just, see you soon."

CHAPTER FOURTEEN

MOLLY HAD BEEN BORED ever since camp had
ended two weeks ago. Okay, Gram had taken her
to the movies and Grandpa had played videogames
with her, but compared to Camp Firefly Wishes, all
that was snore city. At least now things were looking up.

"This is it?" she asked, bouncing on the back
seat as her dad turned into the driveway. She peered
through the gathering darkness, trying to make out
the color of the building. This was too cool. They
were spending the weekend with Miss Rachel. At
her *house!* Cherish had assured her via e-mail that
this was a good sign. Maybe her get-a-new-mom
plan would be a success. Molly crossed her fingers.
She'd just have to keep encouraging things.

"Yep, this is it." Dad eased to a stop.

Molly already had one hand on the door, the
other on the seat belt release.

"Hold it. I want you to remember all the things
we talked about. Good manners, good behavior, all
that?"

Molly rolled her eyes. Like she'd forget to make
a good impression on the woman she wanted for a

mom? "Yes, Dad. You remember your promise, too, right? No calling me Unsinkable and absolutely no disinfecting. You left the spray at home, right? You'll make Miss Rachel feel bad if you do that at her house." And Molly didn't want that. No matter what, she'd be sure her dad made a good impression this weekend, too.

The front door of the duplex opened and the light on the porch flicked on. Miss Rachel stood framed in the right-hand doorway. She waved at them.

Molly grabbed her backpack and tumbled out of the SUV. Dad followed, going around to the back to grab his bag. She raced up the steep porch stairs. "Hi, Miss Rachel. We're here!"

She smiled. "So I see."

"Sorry we're so late. I had appointments tonight, and one quasi-emergency," Dad said.

"Not a problem. I'm glad you could make it. Come on in." She ushered them inside, right into the living room. Miss Rachel's house was tiny compared to theirs. Two archways opened in the opposite wall, one going into a dining room, and the other had a couple of steps up to a little landing. The smell of something yummy drifted through the air. A calico cat jumped off the back of the sofa and whisked past Molly's feet, darting up the stairs.

"Cool! You have a cat."

A funny, strangling noise gurgled low in her father's throat and Molly knew what he was thinking. Cat boxes. Germs.

"That's Peggy Sue. She's not big on people, so don't take it personally."

"What smells so good?" Molly tossed her backpack onto the couch and sniffed the air again.

"I'm making a cake." Miss Rachel turned toward Dad and made an apologetic face. "I hope you don't mind, but there's a picnic tomorrow afternoon at my father's house. My brother, Sloan, is visiting with his two girls, and Dad decided it was a good opportunity for a family get-together. We don't have to go if you don't want, but I thought maybe Molly would like the chance to play with my nieces."

"That's fine. I'd like to meet the man who scared your hair-pulling first-grade teacher." James smiled at her. Meeting her family would go a long way toward satisfying the curiosity he still had, the desire to know everything about her.

Rachel spent the next few minutes giving them a tour. The first floor held the living room, dining room and kitchen, with an enclosed porch that ran along the back of the house. The most interesting feature of the house was the steps. From the living room, there were two up to a little landing, then, if you went straight, two more back down into the kitchen, but if you turned left, you could climb to the second floor. James and Molly had never seen anything quite like it.

"This is where you'll be sleeping, Molly," Rachel said as they passed the bathroom at the top of the stairs. She opened a bedroom door and stepped inside.

Daniel's room. And James was willing to bet she hadn't changed a thing since her son's death. Yet there wasn't a speck of dust on any of the furniture. Either she'd cleaned for their arrival, or she kept the room spotless as a sort of memorial. Light blue walls, a bedspread and matching curtains covered with yellow dump trucks and bulldozers, a short bookshelf that held dozens of children's books. The sight of the Fisher-Price school bus on the top of the shelf kicked James square in the chest. He remembered Daniel's wish: to go to kindergarten on a big yellow bus.

A red sweatshirt lay draped over the top of the oak dresser, and a small pair of sneakers sat on the floor beside the closet as though the young owner might walk through the door at any minute.

Rachel hovered by the bed, hands fluttering nervously before she opted to smooth the pillow. "I'm sorry. It's not exactly a…girlie room." Her voice caught, then she bit down on her lower lip.

James found himself struggling with the overwhelming need to comfort her.

Molly looked up from checking out the bookshelf. "That's okay, Miss Rachel. I like it." She pulled a book off the shelf and waved it in the air. "Jack Prelutsky. I love his poems."

"Me, too." Rachel offered his daughter a tentative smile. "And Shel Silverstein's, too."

"Yeah."

James set Molly's backpack on the floor. "Time for you to brush your teeth and get ready for bed. It's late, and it seems like Rachel has plans for us tomorrow."

"Okay, Dad."

James raised an eyebrow but didn't comment on her uncharacteristic compliance. Downstairs, something beeped.

"My cake." Rachel brushed past him. "Come down when you have Molly settled."

Ten minutes and four Prelutsky poems later, he ambled down the kitchen steps. Passing the fridge, he noticed a painting hung with magnets—a big yellow shape with four black blobs along the bottom. He didn't need the neat, perfectly formed teacher's printing across the top to know it was a school bus and created by Daniel.

Rachel inverted a cake pan over a cooling rack. As she set it on the white countertop, he sidled up behind her and sniffed deeply. "Smells terrific."

"Chocolate cake. I'll make vanilla icing in the morning."

"I was talking about you." He pushed aside her ponytail, dropped his mouth to the back of her neck and nuzzled the soft skin there. "Mmm. I've waited two weeks to do that. And this." Turning her, he wrapped his arms around her waist and drew her flush against him, then kissed her properly.

Rachel's muscles relaxed. She allowed herself to

get lost in the pleasant sensations of his lips on hers, his fingers drifting along her spine. One part of her remained aware, listening for any signs that Molly was still up, but the rest of her let go and simply enjoyed the warmth of this man. When he broke the kiss, she smiled up at him. "It was worth the wait."

"I think so, too." He went on to explain how busy he'd been at his practice, catching up, and giving his partner time off for a vacation of his own. Rachel cleaned up the mess from baking the cake while they chatted. Eventually they moved to the living room. James paused in front of the gas fireplace that occupied the short wall between the two archways. He lifted down the picture frame with Daniel's bronzed baby shoes. The photo showed her little boy in a pair of red-and-green-plaid flannel pajamas in front of a Christmas tree, clutching a teddy bear.

James pointed. "He definitely had his mother's smile."

"That was taken the Christmas before—" Rachel cleared her throat "—before he died. It's my favorite picture of him."

He set it back on the mantel, centering it carefully. Taking her hand, he led her to the sofa. "It's a great picture. Rachel," he said softly, "how often do you clean his room?"

She shook her head and shrugged. "At first, I closed the door and didn't go in there. Didn't let anyone else go in there, either. But on the anniversary of his death, I went in with a package of berry wine coolers and his photo album, got totally plastered and fell asleep on the floor.'' She offered him a wry smile. ''Woke up with the imprint of a Lego block on my cheek. Decided then to tidy up, but I haven't been able to bring myself to get rid of his stuff. Just not—''

''Ready,'' he finished for her, reaching for her hand.

''Right.''

''Well, when you decide you are, if you want some help, or just someone to be there with you…'' He tightened his fingers around hers.

She bit her bottom lip. How had she managed to find a man like this? Exactly where their relationship was going, or how to define it, she didn't know, but for now, she was grateful. ''Thanks.''

The phone rang. Rachel crossed the living room to her oak rolltop desk on the far side. She peered down at the caller-ID and cursed, something far stronger than her usual ''sugar cookies.''

''What's wrong?'' James asked, rising from the sofa.

''It's Roman.'' She grabbed the cordless receiver from the cradle. ''Dammit, Roman, I don't want to talk to you, so quit calling me!'' Jabbing the off button did nothing to placate her annoyance, so she slammed it back into the base.

James wrapped his arms around her from behind.

"You're trembling. How many times has he called since the night we went out for dinner?"

"A couple. Usually hangups on my machine, 'cause even if I'm here, I don't pick it up. But I've had enough."

"Have you talked to the police? Rachel, stalking isn't something to be taken lightly."

"Stalking?" She wriggled from his embrace and turned to face him. "He's not stalking me. Roman isn't like that. An annoying pain in the ass, yes, a stalker, no. He'd never hurt me or anything."

"Then what does he want?"

"I don't know. Jerry said Roman just needs to talk to me."

"Maybe he's trying to come to terms with Daniel's death, too? Looking for some closure?" He stroked her cheek.

Closure? Was that really possible when you'd lost such an important part of your life? Rachel shrugged, as much in answer to her own unasked question as to James's. "I don't know. It's not my problem, is it? I'm busy enough trying to get myself together without worrying about him."

"Well, I'm worried about *you*. If he does seem unbalanced or if he doesn't get the message and stop calling, promise me you'll contact the police?"

Using her index finger, she rubbed gently at the tension lines in his face. "Stop worrying. I'll be fine." The mantel clock softly chimed eleven. "It's late. Since you've insisted on sleeping down here on the sofa bed—''

James groaned. "Rachel, I'd love nothing more than to share your bed upstairs, but not—''

"With Molly in the house." She pressed her lips briefly against his mouth. "I know, and I understand." Understood, but she didn't like it. The idea of spending the whole night in his arms was not only erotic, but strangely comforting. "I was just teasing you. I'll be back with some pillows. I put clean sheets and blankets on the bed this afternoon."

When she returned with his sleeping supplies, she paused on the landing, enjoying the view as he smoothed out the bedding on the sofa.

He straightened up and turned, catching her watching him. She dropped the pillows on the end of the bed, then crooked her finger. "Give me something to think about all night, 'cause I doubt I'll be sleeping, knowing you're down here."

The kiss he gave her definitely qualified as something to think about. Dream about.

"WHAT ARE YOUR INTENTIONS toward my daughter?" Steven Thompson pointed a metal spatula at James's chest, brandishing the cooking tool in a confident manner that implied he expected a satisfactory answer. Burgers sizzled on the grill, their pleasant aroma filling this little corner of Steven's backyard. James realized that being asked to help cook meant a grilling for him, as well as the food.

His silver-white hair in a short buzz cut, and still fit and trim with muscular shoulders, the Sarge reminded James of Richard Dean Anderson from *Stargate*.

"Sir?" The respect came automatically. Hell, Rachel's father carried himself in such a way that you couldn't help but want to snap to attention and salute. No wonder she'd kept so much emotion hidden in order to please this man.

"You have a daughter, James. I'm sure you can understand a father's desire to protect his little girl." Genuine concern filled the man's hazel eyes, then was quickly replaced with a stern expression designed to intimidate. Not that it did. The psychologist in James had this man's number. He loved his daughter tremendously, and this was his way of showing it.

"I can understand wanting to protect your child, yes."

"Good. Because my daughter's been through a lot lately, and I'd hate to see her hurt again." Steven's jaw set in a firm line, and he returned his attention to the burgers.

"I have no intention of hurting her, sir."

"No one ever does."

"Where's Rachel?" Sloan, Rachel's older brother, trotted up onto the brick patio, face lined with tension. He had darker hair than his sister, but they shared the same blue eyes. And right now, they were sparking with mixed anger and anxiety.

"I think she's in the house with Molly and Ashley, putting the finishing touches on the cake."

"Why?" James asked.

"Because Roman just drove up."

Steven cursed and shoved the spatula into James's hands. "I'll take care of this." He briskly strode from the patio, Sloan on his heels.

James slapped the metal tool onto the redwood picnic table and raced after the other men. Did they know Roman had been hassling Rachel? He darted around Sloan's four-door pickup with Texas plates and pulled up short at the driver's door of the Goat. The two Thompson men stood near the front bumper, arms folded across their chests. Between father and son, there was enough muscle and testosterone to more than take care of one ex-husband.

"Sarge. Sloan." Roman removed his wraparound sunglasses and slipped them into the pocket of his suit jacket. With his shoulder-length dark hair neatly pulled back into a short ponytail, the man was not what James had expected. He had a bad-boy aura that didn't mesh with the sweet image of Rachel. No wonder her father had wanted to know James's intentions. This man was the total antithesis of Rachel. James moved forward to stand at Steven's other shoulder.

Roman held out his hands. "Look, guys, I don't

want any trouble. I'm just here to talk to Rachel. Five minutes, that's all I need."

"You've got five seconds to get your ass out of here before I kick the shit out of it." Steven popped his knuckles, either in warning or preparation.

Sloan rolled his neck. "I don't think my sister has anything to say to you anymore, Roman."

A blue Taurus squealed to a halt at the curb. The front door popped open, and a man with a rolling gait, more of a hobble than a limp, rushed toward them. "Roman! What the hell are you doing?"

The dark man turned. "Trying to talk to Rachel, Uncle Jer, just like you told me to."

"Here? Do you have a death wish or are you just plain crazy?"

Roman shook his head. "Neither. Forget it." He yanked his sunglasses back out of his pocket and jammed them on his face. "I've got a business meeting out of town. I'll be gone for a few days. I'll call you when I get back." Stiffly, he stalked to a charcoal Lincoln Town Car. He pulled away from the curb and took off at high speed.

"You gotta do something about him, Jerry, or I'm going to," Steven said.

"He really needs to talk to her, Sarge. I swear to you, I have Rachel's best interests at heart. You know I love her, too. I wouldn't BS you."

"Does this have anything to do with Daniel?" James asked.

They all turned to look at him as though he'd

appeared out of nowhere. Steven shook his head. "I don't give a damn what it has to do with. I will not allow that man to upset my daughter any further."

Sloan and Jerry nodded. After a moment, James did, too. Rachel's father was not a man to be argued with. But the psychologist in James couldn't help thinking that confronting Roman might be good for Rachel. Especially if she could do it where her family—and James—could support and protect her.

MOLLY WATCHED BROOK THOMPSON apply makeup, torn between envy and horror. Green eye shadow only accentuated the silver stud poking through Miss Rachel's niece's eyebrow. And the black lipstick…yuck. "Did it hurt a lot to get your eyebrow pierced?"

"Of course it did." The girl globbed on mascara.

"So why'd you do it?"

The thirteen-year-old laid the tube on the dresser and glanced at Molly in the mirror. "To get my father's attention."

"Did it work?" Sheesh, Molly was always trying to avoid her father's attention. Molly and Brook had quickly discovered a common bond—the lack of a mother. Brook's mother had been killed in a car accident three years ago. She and her little sister, Ashley, who was only four now, lived in Texas with their father.

"Yeah. He went through the roof." Brook smirked.

"Do you wish you had a mother?" Molly rolled over onto her stomach on the double bed in the small but tidy guest room Brook was sharing with Ashley. Propping her chin on her palms, she kicked her feet in the air.

"Hell, no. What would I want another mother for?" Brook scowled.

"I want one. I'm hoping Miss Rachel can be my new mom."

"You know what my father says?" Brook whirled to face her.

Molly shook her head.

"Be careful what you wish for. You just might get it."

"So? Why should I be upset if I get Miss Rachel for a mom? I like her. She's cool."

Brook's laugh was sharp. "Mental case is more like it. Besides, you don't want to be part of our family. We tend to lose people. My grandma, my mother, my cousin, Daniel... We're hard on family around here. It's a curse."

"That's just stupid. Sometimes people die."

"That's right, tiger. Sometimes they do," her dad said softly from the doorway. "And it hurts. But we have to keep moving forward. And speaking of moving forward, lunch is ready. You need to wash up."

Molly scrambled from the bed, hoping her dad

hadn't overheard the start of that conversation. He wasn't supposed to know that she'd wished for Miss Rachel to be her new mom. "Okay, Dad."

"Your father said for you to come down, too, Brook."

"Whatever." Brook moved back to the dresser. "I'll be there when I get there."

Molly followed her father into the hallway, realizing that despite his stupid cleaning stuff, and all that, her dad was a pretty cool guy and she was lucky to have him.

With Miss Rachel, they'd make a complete family.

And everything would be perfect.

SHRIEKS OF CHILDREN'S laughter rang across the backyard. Several of the neighborhood kids—three boys and a girl—had come over. After a spoon-and-potato race, organized by Sloan, the group was now involved in a lively game of tag. Molly appeared to be having a great time. Brook watched from the sideline, doing her best to appear nonchalant, but sometimes not able to keep the longing from her green-shaded eyes.

James and Sloan had commiserated on how hard it was to raise girls by themselves, and Rachel's brother had warned him that things only got worse, that the terrible teens made the terrible twos look like a cakewalk.

Little Ashley was conked out on her dad's lap.

Sloan cradled his younger daughter against his chest, absentmindedly stroking her chestnut hair. All the adults were slumped in lawn chairs on the edge of the patio.

"I still can't get over it," Jerry muttered.

"Over what?" Rachel asked.

"The fact that little Molly has had a heart transplant." Jerry faced James. "I'd never have known."

"Thanks. She's doing great."

Jerry leaned over and grasped Rachel's hand. "See? Aren't you glad that you donated Daniel's organs? Somewhere out there are kids who can run and play today because of what you did."

"Yeah, Jer. I'm glad." Rachel gave his fingers a quick squeeze, then pulled her hand free. But she wasn't. Nothing could ease the pain in her own heart, the wish that Daniel still ran through his grandfather's backyard with the neighbor kids. She could feel her father's intense gaze on her.

She pinched the bridge of her nose. Rising from the chair, she headed for the picnic table. "I think I'll take a few of these things back into the house and put them away." The mustard bottle tipped over as she reached for the leftover potato salad.

"I'll help." James followed her into the kitchen, arms laden with the condiments and the cake. He plunked them down on the counter, removed the big plastic bowl from her arms, and set that down, too. He pulled her into an embrace. "Are you okay?"

"Fine," she mumbled against his chest, content to once again draw comfort from his strength.

"No, you're not. Every time you get upset, you do that thing with your nose."

"What thing?" She tilted her head and looked at him.

"This thing." He gently pinched the upper portion of her nose.

Rachel offered him a halfhearted smile. "Busted. You're very observant, counselor."

"Is there anything I can do for you, Rachel?"

"Actually, yes. Would you…I haven't been to Daniel's grave in a while, and I don't want to go alone. Would you go with me?"

His eyes widened, as if she'd knocked the breath right out of him. "I…uh—"

"Never mind."

"No, no, I'll go with you. It's just…what about Molly? I'd really rather not take her."

"She can stay here with the kids. My father and Sloan will watch her. We won't be gone long. The cemetery is only about ten minutes from here. Please?"

He exhaled deeply. "Okay. Let's go."

CHAPTER FIFTEEN

A LIGHT BREEZE RUSTLED the pair of Mylar balloons Rachel clutched in her hand as James followed her from the car. One balloon bore the words *I Love You;* the other had a truck on it. Flowers, Rachel had explained, were for girls in Daniel's opinion, so she always brought balloons when she visited. The small cemetery on the outskirts of town had an understanding caretaker and few rules when it came to gifts left at gravesites.

He followed her silently as they moved among the headstones. Birds chirped in the nearby trees, and though the hot summer sun beat down on them, goose bumps rose on James's arms.

Rachel stopped in front of a blue-gray, roughly rectangular marble monument. The sides curved, and a heart was hewn in the upper left corner. She stooped and threaded the ribbons from the balloons through a slit in the stone along the bottom portion of the heart.

James began to squat beside her, but a small package in his pocket jabbed him in the thigh. He withdrew the purchase he'd made downtown from the little all-purpose store while Rachel had been occupied with selecting Daniel's balloons. "Hey there, Daniel."

In his mind's eye, he could see the smiling boy from the picture on her mantel. A lump swelled in his throat as the true impact of Rachel's loss stormed him. This child, *her* child, had been one who'd laughed and loved, played and slept…and in his final rest, had given others another chance at life. He cleared his throat and forced the words past his strangled vocal chords. "I brought you something, buddy."

He set the tiny yellow school bus on the monument's base.

"Oh, James."

He turned to look at her. Her lower lip quivered, and she covered her mouth with a trembling hand. Tears welled up in her eyes, but she made no attempt to stop them. They spilled over and trickled down her face. She rose to her feet.

He stood and gathered her into his arms. "I am so sorry, Rachel," he murmured into her hair.

Sheltered against his chest, Rachel let the tears flow.

He'd brought Daniel a school bus.

In that moment, she realized she loved him. James. The man who'd taught her it was okay to cry. Who'd taught her what it was to live again.

And she loved Molly, his courageous, spunky, hell-of-a-kid kid.

Rachel bit her lower lip in an effort to stem not

the tears, not the grief, but the sudden and over-whelming fear that followed the revelation she was in love with both father and child.

She'd barely survived losing Daniel.

Would she survive losing again? Molly's trans-planted heart left her at risk.

Hospitals. The word brought the cloying scents and rush of further terror. Loving Molly and James would automatically mean confronting hospitals and doctors.

Rachel wasn't sure she could do that.

SEVERAL DAYS LATER, armed with a pair of empty cardboard boxes and some strapping tape, Rachel paused in the entrance to Daniel's room.

She set the supplies on his bed, then moved to his dresser, skimming her fingertips over the oak leaves carved into the surface. She sighed, then started with the bottom drawer, pulling out jeans, which went into the box to be given away. The army sweatshirt given to Daniel by her father went into the to-be-saved box.

Quickly and methodically, she made short work of the dresser.

The cat brushed against Rachel's ankle. She bent and scooped her up, stroking the soft fur. "I know, Peggy Sue. It's weird, isn't it? But we have to clean this up. I want to start the new school year looking forward." Peggy Sue purred and rubbed her head against Rachel's chin.

The sound of a car in the driveway came through the open bedroom window. She moved to brush aside the curtain. "Damn."

Peggy Sue still clutched against her chest, Rachel flew down the stairs and flung open the front door just as her ex-husband climbed to the top of the porch steps. "Roman. What the hell are you doing here?"

Roman held up his hands. "Rachel, please. I just need five minutes of your time, then I'm out of your life for good."

"I thought you were out of my life for good after Daniel's funeral."

The steel-gray eyes darkened. He blinked quickly several times. "Rae, I know you blame me for what happened to Daniel. Hell, most of the time, *I* blame me. But it was an accident. I swear, I looked away for just a minute—"

"So you could kiss the bimbo."

"Well..." His face flushed. "That's true. Believe me, if I could change it, I would."

"Why are you here? You didn't come here just to ask my forgiveness, did you? It's a little late for that." Rachel lowered the squirming cat to the floor and stepped out onto the porch as Peggy Sue took off toward the kitchen.

Roman climbed the final step. "I...have something to tell you. I wanted to tell you myself." He leaned against the banister and stared at her. "What have you been doing? You've got a big piece of tape stuck to your arm.'' He pointed.

Rachel ripped the tape off without flinching, even though it yanked out about a million tiny hairs. Weakness would not be displayed in front of this man. ''If you must know, I was packing up some of Daniel's things.''

Roman's mouth opened, then closed. The tiny muscle on the side of his jaw twitched. ''Are you getting rid of everything?''

She shook her head. ''Of course not.''

''If you come across that baseball mitt I gave him for his birthday, I'd...'' Roman turned his head away from her, staring at the company-furnished Lincoln in the driveway. ''I'd like to have it,'' he finished in a choked voice.

''Uh. Sure.'' She silently cursed the softening in her chest, the acknowledgement that Roman actually felt pain over losing Daniel. That had been *her* exclusive territory. But as Daniel's father, he was as entitled to feel loss as she was. And Rachel should be relieved to discover that he did feel something. *This* was the man she'd initially been attracted to. The man who'd given her Daniel. ''I'll set it aside for you when I find it.''

''Thanks.''

For a few moments they simply stood on the porch, listening to the wind rustle the leaves. Finally, Roman cleared his throat again and turned to face her. "Rachel, I'm getting married again. To Clarissa. This weekend."

"Oh." Slowly his words sank in. There was a flash of anger over the fact that he was moving on, but it was short-lived. She silently thanked James for the fact that she felt no jealousy. He'd made her feel every inch a desirable woman. "Well, thanks for telling me."

He took another step toward her. "That's not all of it." Guilt filled his face.

She'd seen that look before. "Oh. My. God." From nowhere, a combat boot struck firmly in her gut, as understanding dawned. "No," she whispered. "Don't tell me she's pregnant."

Roman inclined his head.

"I guess you didn't figure out not to buy your condoms here in town!" she yelled. "Don't learn from your mistakes, huh, Roman?"

"Daniel wasn't a mistake, Rachel. And this baby isn't, either."

Rachel searched the porch for something, anything, to hurl at his head, but came up empty. "You bastard! You son of a bitch!" She slumped against the front door for support. She'd been packing her baby's life into boxes, and he'd been making another one.

A black pickup truck roared right onto the front lawn, crushing the green blades of grass. Her father jumped out of the passenger side, and Sloan swung down from the driver's.

The troops had arrived. And she'd never been happier to see her family.

"I thought I told you to stay away from my daughter?" Her father grabbed Roman by the shirt and dragged him down the stairs.

"Easy, Sarge." Roman regained his balance, and again held his hands up in a gesture of supplication. "I told her what I needed to tell her. I'm going now." He turned back toward her. "I'm sorry, Rae. I never meant to hurt you."

Rachel, her father and her brother watched, motionless, until Roman drove away.

"How did you know?" Rachel asked.

Sloan pointed at the opposite side of the duplex. "Mrs. Benton called Dad when she saw Roman pull in."

Rachel waved her thanks to the woman, her landlady and friend, who nodded and dropped the curtain back in place.

"You okay, sis?" Sloan gathered her into a hug. "What the hell was so important he had to tell you in person?"

Rachel briefly squeezed her brother, then backed from his embrace. Her father watched her carefully. She pinched the bridge of her nose. Good soldiers didn't cry. "Oh, not much. Just that he's getting married again." Her stomach churned. "And... having another baby."

"Why, that..." Her father launched into a series

of words Rachel had learned early her dad could use, but she couldn't repeat. His hands curled into fists.

"You want us to flatten him for you, Rae?" Sloan offered her a quick grin, but he wasn't teasing.

She shook her head. "He's not worth a jail sentence, that's for sure. Besides—" she ran her fingers down Sloan's arm, desperate to connect with someone, aching from holding inside the whirlwind of emotion she wanted to let go "—in his own way, Roman's hurting, too. I just didn't realize it before now."

The muffled sound of the ringing phone came through the front door. "I have to get that. Come in, guys. You want some lunch?"

"No, thanks," Sloan said. "If you're okay, we should run. We left the kids alone. I know at thirteen Brook should be able to watch Ashley for a few minutes, but these days, I just don't know what she's fixin' to do next."

Anxiety and tension showed in her brother's blue eyes. How had she missed that before? Too busy with her own problems to see those of the people around her, the people who mattered to her. She made a resolution to sit down with Sloan and have a long talk.

Talking was good. James said so.

Oh, James. Rachel's throat constricted as the impact of Roman's news hit her again. Somehow she didn't think talking would be enough to ease this pain.

JAMES PACED IN THE restaurant's parking lot, along the side of his SUV. Off to the north, dark clouds filled the sky, but the storms hadn't materialized yet. He checked his watch again. Unless he'd miscalculated, Rachel should have arrived by now. Maybe the weather had already turned near her and she was driving through rain.

He hadn't been able to keep her off his mind since returning home from her house on Sunday night. And when his appointments had canceled without warning, leaving him with an open afternoon, he hadn't been able to resist calling her and suggesting that they meet "halfway" at Grove City for a late lunch.

Impulsive. Totally out of character for him.

And damn if it didn't feel good.

He scanned the traffic exiting 79 from the north. The familiar shape of the Goat came off the ramp and got trapped at the light. Just a few minutes later, the black car rumbled into a parking space beside his.

She jumped out. Before he could even offer a greeting, he found himself pressed against the SUV, Rachel's mouth desperately seeking his.

Taken off guard, he fumbled awkwardly before

responding in kind, wrapping his arms around her and kissing her deeply.

"Woo-hoo! Go man!"

James came up for air as a car of college kids cruised by, one hanging out the back window, giving him a thumbs-up.

He didn't care for the way they were scanning her. He glanced down at Rachel. Her eyes were dark and intense. "You hungry?"

She nodded. "But not for food."

Yeah, he'd gotten that message already. His body made it clear it found the idea appealing.

"We could get a room over there," Rachel whispered, shrugging a shoulder in the direction of the motel across the street.

"Are you sure that's what you want?" He ran his fingers over her cheek. A pale pink flush appeared beneath his strokes.

"Yes."

Without another word, they crossed the road, and in less than fifteen minutes, they'd checked in and stood just outside the room.

James slipped the magnetic card through the slot. Rachel brushed by him. As he entered behind her, she turned and pressed him against the closed door.

Rational thought fled in the wake of her kisses. Her fingers fumbled with the buttons on his shirt, then she yanked the tails from his jeans. Her tongue swirled around his nipple, then trailed heat across his chest. "Jeez, Rachel. You trying to kill me?"

"Hardly. You make me feel alive," she murmured against his navel. "I need to feel alive."

When she popped the button over his zipper, he groaned and grabbed her by the arms, hauling her up.

Fueled by her desire, he removed her T-shirt and tossed it to the floor. He caressed her breasts through the lace-covered white bra, kissed the curve of her neck as she arched backward, a blatant invitation.

Their ragged breathing filled his ears. The unique scent of Rachel—lemons, sunshine, life—spurred his need for her. Soon they both stood naked, clothing strewn haphazardly on the floor. She fitted her body against his, the hardened tips of her breasts pressing against his chest, the juncture of her thighs cradling the base of his erection.

She dragged her toes up his calf, settled her knee against his hip, totally opening herself to him.

"Rachel, not so fast—"

"Yes! I need you, James," she cried.

"Not here, not like this. At least on the bed."

She dropped her leg and grabbed his hand, pulling him across the room to the king-size bed. Without bothering to draw back the covers, she pressed him onto his back, then straddled him. He groaned. "You *are* trying to kill me. Rachel, wait."

"I can't." She brushed her body over his.

"At least let me get—" His words dissolved into a low moan as she joined them together.

Thunder rumbled outside, and streaks of lightning illuminated the room as the skies opened up.

Rain pounded against the windows as she drew comfort from loving him.

Rachel trembled as her orgasm approached, then quickly overtook her. "Oh, James!"

In a flash, he rolled her over, driving into her with the intensity she craved. After several more strokes, he pulled out, leaving her empty and incomplete. His erection pressed against her belly. "Rachel," he moaned in her ear, then shuddered.

Her cheeks flamed as she realized what he'd done.

What *she'd* done. She bit her lower lip. Her hands flew to his shoulders and pushed at him.

Hurt and a million questions floated in his eyes, increasing her guilt, magnifying her embarrassment. He shifted to the side and slipped off her.

She bolted for the bathroom.

Leaving James alone, puzzling over her behavior. After several minutes, during which he recovered his normal breathing, James pulled back the covers and settled into the bed. A little while later, the bathroom door opened, and he heard a faint, strangled squeak.

"If you're looking for your clothes, you can forget about it," he called to her. "I'm holding them hostage. So, just come back to bed and explain to me what the hell that was all about."

She appeared hesitantly, a white towel wrapped around her body. She pinched the bridge of her nose. "I'm sorry," she whispered.

"Aw, dammit, Rachel." He jumped up and went to take her in his arms. "What's going on, huh?"

Forehead pressed against his shoulder, she shook her head.

"Come lie with me. Let me hold you."

He guided her back to the bed and climbed in, once more pulling her into his arms. "Now, tell me what's going on. You didn't sound right when I called you, and now I know something's up."

Outside the sheer curtains over the window, thunder rolled and lightning flashed as he waited for her to answer. Finally she spoke softly. "I started packing Daniel's things today."

"By yourself?"

"Yes."

"Rachel, you don't have to do everything by yourself. Sometimes it's okay to ask for help. I told you I'd be there for you."

Love is being there for the hard stuff.

Her words from the night of their dinner date came back to him.

And kicked him right in the middle of the chest. He was in *love* with her.

What had started as a fantasy, turned into a live-in-the-moment summer fling, now the relationship had taken an even more serious turn.

"There's more," Rachel said.

"More?"

Her fingers swirled across his chest as she nodded. "Roman came to see me today."

James tensed. "And?"

"He…he had some news. He's getting married again. This weekend." She sniffled.

A cold sensation invaded his body. Why did it matter to her if her ex got married again? "How does that make you feel?"

"How does that make me feel?" She sat up, clutching the cotton sheet to her chest with one hand despite the fact that she still wore the towel. She slapped him on the shoulder. "Don't you turn into a counselor on me now! I need a friend, not a shrink!"

"A friend can ask you how you feel about your ex-husband getting married again." *Especially a friend who's suddenly discovered much deeper feelings for you.*

"I'm mad, that's how I feel!"

"Not jealous?"

"Hell no!" Her ramrod-straight posture slowly dissolved, her shoulders and back slumping. "At least, not about the getting married part." Her bottom lip quivered, and she bit down on it.

"There's still more?"

She nodded. "He's—" her voice faded to a barely audible whisper "—having another baby."

"Oh, Rachel." Now, that really explained her behavior. Especially the fact that she'd ignored her own obsession about birth control. He drew her down next to him and rolled to his side, propping himself on his elbow. "You know another baby isn't going to replace Daniel, right? Nothing will ever replace him, not with you, and not with Roman, either.''

"I used you. I…I jumped your bones.''

He laughed. ''You don't hear me complaining, do you? Being used for sex by a beautiful woman is every guy's fantasy. Although—'' he sobered instantly ''—what are the odds we just made a baby of our own, Rachel? I mean, I protected you… us…the best I could, but—''

"The timing's not right. We should be fine.''

James wrestled with a surge of disappointment. And realized in that moment exactly *how* serious he was about this woman. He wanted more than just a summer fling. More than weekends with her.

But could they have more? Could she be a real mother to Molly? Or would the pressure of dealing with a child with Molly's medical history eventually send her bolting?

"Are you mad at me?'' Her fingers glided along his jawline.

"No, I'm not mad at you.'' He turned his head, planted a kiss on her palm. ''But maybe we need to talk about a few things.'' He looked at her. ''Rachel, do you remember at the restaurant? I asked what was the most pleasurable thing you could imagine me doing to you?''

She nodded. ''I sure do.''

"Can you picture it again?''

"Mmm-hmm.'' She shut her eyes, and her smile

turned to pure sensuality as she took his reawakening erection in her hand.

He leaned closer to her ear, did his best to pitch his voice in a soothing tone. Not easy, considering all he wanted to do was groan. "Good. I want to talk to you about what happened at the hospital that night."

She stilled.

"It's just like the lasagna, Rachel. It's a conditioned response, that's all. One we can overcome together. It might not be easy…" His words trailed as she released him and rolled over onto her back. "Rachel? Please look at me."

She turned her head.

"Rachel, I'm in love with you."

Her eyes widened.

"I need to know that you're willing to work on this hospital phobia."

"Oh, James. I…I'm afraid."

"Of what, exactly?"

She looked away from him. "Of…loving you. And Molly." Her voice rasped, thick with emotion. "And…I do love you. Both of you. But I'm also afraid of how I feel when you just say the word *hospital.*"

"And how do you feel?"

She took a deep breath. Tremors rocked along her skin where she lay pressed against him. "My heart pounds and my palms get all sweaty. I'm not sure if I'm hot or cold."

"It's just anxiety, sweetie. We can get through it." Her expression seemed doubtful. "Let me show you." He grinned. "I'll make it worth your while."

"O-okay. I'll try."

"That's all I ask." He lowered his head and nuzzled her neck, trailing his fingers along her thigh. "Hospital," he murmured softly as he stroked her.

She sighed—an encouraging sound that was more pleasure than distress. "Just tell me you don't use this method with your patients."

He laughed. "Hell, no. For one thing, I'd like to keep my license."

"And for another?" She gasped as he continued to tease her.

"I only want to be this way with you." He smiled. Rachel had more strength than she realized. Given time, she could overcome all her fears.

He'd found that very, very special lady he'd told Molly would be so hard to come by. And maybe a second chance at love and a future, too.

CHAPTER SIXTEEN

THE FOLLOWING FRIDAY NIGHT found Rachel snuggled into the recliner portion of James's blue sectional sofa, Molly cuddled up against her as they watched a DVD of a recent movie. James was in his office, taking a phone call from a patient. A large bowl of popcorn was balanced on Rachel's lap. Molly giggled as they both reached into it at the same time and bumped hands.

"Sorry," the little girl said. "Looks like I'm still bumping into you."

Rachel chuckled. "Guess so. But that's okay. I'll always be glad to have you bump into me."

Molly snuggled closer, rested her head on Rachel's shoulder.

God, it felt so right. Guiltily she realized she hadn't even thought of Daniel since she'd arrived at James's restored Victorian house for her weekend stay.

The closing credits of the film rolled across the wide-screen TV and music blared from James's surround-sound stereo system.

Molly sighed. "I love that story." She wiggled out of the recliner to grab the remote from the glass-

and-oak coffee table. Silence replaced the theme song. "Hey, you wanna see more pictures?" she asked.

"Sure," Rachel said. Anything to distract herself from thinking about whether or not this scene—she, James and Molly together—was right, or a big mistake on Rachel's part.

Molly's floppy-eared bunny slippers scuffed against the tan carpet as she crossed to the bookcases behind the sofa.

Rachel moved the plastic bowl from her lap to the table. Molly plopped a photo album in its place on Rachel's lap. "Here." She climbed back into the recliner and snuggled close again. "My gram made this for me." She opened to the first page, and Rachel caught her breath.

"This is me when I was just born."

A tiny infant lay in an isolette, wires and tubes connected to the fragile-looking body. Rachel tried to ignore the sudden change in the living room's temperature.

"I had my first surgery the next day." Molly flipped the page. "Here's Dad holding me a few days after that."

A much-younger James, clad in a yellow protective gown, showed off his daughter for the camera. Tiffany was nowhere to be seen. Although, maybe she'd been the one taking the pictures. Rachel would give the woman the benefit of the doubt. For the first time, she realized exactly how difficult those early years with Molly must have been.

And she understood why, when he'd confessed his love to her, his first concern had been her hospital phobia.

Molly quickly skimmed through a bunch of pages. "Here's me and Cherish, when we were both waiting for our new hearts."

Rachel's chest tightened at the sight of the two girls she'd known only as mischievous, active kids looking pale and exhausted, wearing hospital pj's in identical beds. Her throat constricted, and she said a silent prayer that neither girl ever looked like that again.

"Molly?" James appeared in the archway that led to the foyer.

"Yeah, Dad?"

"Time for bed. Go upstairs and brush your teeth. I'll be up in a few minutes to tuck you in."

"Do I have to?"

"Yes, you have to. Now, scoot."

"Okay." She slid off the sofa, leaving an empty cold spot along Rachel's side.

"Miss Rachel?"

Rachel looked up from the album to the child's face. A healthy, happy face, a far cry from the one in the photo.

Rachel smiled. Somewhere there was another child whose face now looked healthy because she had agreed to donate her son's heart.

Finally, that thought offered her some comfort. "What, Molly?"

"Will you come up with Dad and help tuck me in?"

She looked over at James, who nodded his approval. "Sure I will, honey."

"Okay, tiger, enough stalling. Move it."

"I'm going." Molly skipped from the room

James ruffled her hair as she passed him, then he came and sank down on to the sofa next to Rachel. "Sorry about being gone so long, but it's my weekend on-call."

"That's okay."

"What are you reading?" He glanced at the book. "Oh." He edged closer to her, replacing the warmth from his daughter with his own, helping to ward off the chill. "You do realize that's a picture of my kid in the *hospital,* right?"

The pages slapped together as she closed the album. "You just had to point that part out, didn't you?" She shivered.

"Yep. It's a good step, Rachel. I'm proud of you." He pressed his lips to her cheek.

Okay, so she wouldn't tell him her stomach was doing the Macarena dance. They'd move forward one small step at a time.

THEY'D PLANNED TO SPEND a quiet day at home. But James had been called away to a patient crisis. Rachel was happy that he'd been comfortable leaving Molly in her care.

Molly drew back the long curtain from the window and looked out. "See that park across the street?"

Rachel nodded.

"I used to sit here a lot, watching the kids play out there, and wishing I could play with them."

"But you couldn't because...they had germs?" Rachel tickled the bottom of Molly's foot, and the little girl giggled.

"No, because I was too tired. Daddy or Grandpa used to carry me up the stairs a lot. Now look at me." She grinned at Rachel. "I had fun at your house last week." Her pigtails bounced as she sat back up abruptly. "I wish I had known Daniel. I'll bet he was fun, like you."

Memories of her little boy playing cars on the living room rug played out in Rachel's mind. She pressed her lips together, then realized Molly was waiting for an answer. "Yeah. We had good times together."

"Don't be sad, Miss Rachel." Molly scrambled off the window seat and crossed over to her desk. The middle drawer screeched in protest as she yanked it out and pulled something from the depths. "I made you something."

Rachel swung her legs off the side of the bench. "What's that, sweetie?"

Molly dropped her gaze to the floor. "This." She

pulled her hands from behind her back and held the offering out to Rachel. "It's like the ones we made at camp. Only I made this one specially for you."

"Thank you." Rachel accepted the construction paper firefly. The body was shaped from Molly's foot, and the wings were her hands, with the fingers in pairs and the thumbs tucked underneath. Rachel had come up with the idea at camp after the gift of fireflies from this sweet child.

"Read what I wrote on it."

The corny little poem was Rachel's other part of the project, and it included an empty space for the child to write down a wish. In very neat printing, Molly had written: I wish for Miss Rachel to be my new mom.

Hopeful hazel eyes stared at her.

"Oh, Molly. That's so sweet." She set the project on the cushion beside her and opened her arms. Molly moved into them as if it was the most natural thing in the world. Rachel held her close, felt the reassuring thump of Molly's heart beating against her chest.

"We could be a real family," the little girl said softly. "You wouldn't be alone anymore."

"Honey, I think you might be jumping the gun a little. Your dad and I haven't known each other for all that long—"

Molly backed from her embrace. "So? Nolan said he knew he was going to marry Cherish's mom from the first time they met. You love my dad, right?''

''I care very much about him, yes.''

''And me?'' The lower lip on the freckled face quivered.

''Yes, definitely you!'' Rachel gathered the uncertain child back into her arms. ''You, Molly McClain, are an amazing kid, and very easy to love.''

''My mom didn't think so.''

The pain in the child's voice tore into Rachel's heart. It wouldn't be right to vocalize the uncharitable thoughts she was having about Molly's mother, so she just said, ''Well, *I* do.''

Laughter from the children on the playground across the street entered through the partially opened window. Molly's warm body pressed tightly against hers, and Rachel realized how very right it felt.

Could she love James and Molly and live in each moment with them, not worrying about the future, but enjoying the present?

A loud buzzing noise came from downstairs.

''I'll bet that's our pizza.'' Rachel reluctantly let go of Molly. ''Shall we go see?''

''You go ahead. I'll be right there.'' She plopped down into the chair in front of the desk and offered Rachel an enormous grin, one that flashed the partially showing new tooth on the side. ''I just remembered, I have to e-mail Cherish about something.''

''Okay, but don't be long.''

At the bottom of the stairs, Rachel retrieved her purse from beneath the small phone table as the doorbell rang again. ''I'm coming,'' she yelled. After paying the teenage delivery boy, Rachel turned into the house, shutting the door with a backward bump from her foot. ''Molly! Pepperoni pizza's here!''

''Hey, Miss Rachel! Watch this!'' At the top of the stairs, the girl threw one leg over the highly polished oak banister.

''No! That's not a good idea. I'm sure your father wouldn't approve.'' Rachel headed for the bottom of the stairs, pizza box balanced in her arms, purse slung over her shoulder.

Molly stuck out her lower lip in an exaggerated pout. ''But you're much more fun than he is.'' And she climbed onto the railing. With a shriek of laughter, she flew down the top half. As she came to the curved section near the landing, she wobbled.

Rachel's heart stopped.

So did the entire universe.

Except for Molly.

In painfully slow motion—something Rachel thought only happened in bad movies—Molly went over the railing.

Rachel dropped the pizza. Arms outstretched, she dashed toward the falling child. Like a rag doll,

Molly bounced off the phone table. She hit the parquet wooden floor with an ominous, hollow thud.

"Molly!" Rachel fell to her knees beside the little girl. Checked for breathing and a pulse. Blessedly found them. "Molly? Do you hear me?"

A low moan was the only response.

Rachel dragged the phone to her side by yanking on the cord. "Don't move, honey. I'm getting help."

CHAPTER SEVENTEEN

THE CHATTER OF TOO MANY people and the squeal from radios bore down on Rachel. Red and blue lights from the emergency vehicles outside strobed through the windows. The tightness in her chest wouldn't let go, and breathing was difficult. She tried to process the fireman's questions and at the same time look around him to see what they were doing to Molly. Paramedics leaned over the small form still on the floor. "You told them about her heart, right?" she asked.

"Yes, ma'am. They're keeping a close eye on her, don't you worry. Now, do you have another number where we could try to reach her father?"

She shook her throbbing head. "I've given you all the numbers I have!" She clasped her hands together, both to keep them still and in silent prayer. Nobody had been able to reach James. "You called her grandparents, right?"

At that moment, Liz and Tom McClain, James's parents, burst through the front door. "Molly!" Liz cried, moving to her granddaughter's side. "Gram's here now." She flashed a paper at one of the emer-

gency workers. "I have legal permission to autho-
rize any care she needs."

Tom came toward Rachel. "What happened?"

In a choking voice, she explained the situation.
"I told her not to do it. I'm so sorry!" Her composure broke and hot tears trickled down her face.
This was not the way she had planned her first
meeting with his parents.

"Hey, now." James's father gathered her into his
arms despite the fact they were still virtual strangers. "It's not your fault. There's a reason they call
them accidents."

Her tears became a flood as she wondered if
James would react the same way. Or would he
blame her for his daughter's injuries? The way
she'd blamed Roman for Daniel's.

"I want Miss Rachel!" a small voice cut through
all the chaos.

She'd never heard sweeter words in her life. Rachel shifted from Tom's embrace, wiping her
cheeks with the back of her hand.

She pressed through the throng of people to the
stretcher where they'd placed Molly. She gripped
the little girl's fingers and tried not to look at the
bandage on her head, or the thin arm in a splint.
"I'm here, Molly."

"Stay with me."

Rachel stumbled to keep up with them as they
carried Molly to the waiting ambulance. In the twi-
light, a group of neighbors had gathered on the

sidewalk. The atmosphere grew oppressive with every step Rachel took closer to the emergency vehicle. She pressed her hand to her mouth as they lifted Molly and placed her inside.

Visions of Daniel being loaded into a similar vehicle crowded her mind. The scent of antiseptic drifted from the back. She couldn't get any air. She felt one of the firemen laying a hand on her back. "Miss? Are you all right?"

She shook her head. "Can't…breathe." She moved toward the bumper of the ambulance. "Need to go with her." Light-headed, she swayed.

The fireman grabbed her by the arm. "You're not going anywhere right now."

Liz climbed up next to the paramedic. "I'll ride with her."

"I'll follow in the car," Tom said.

"I want Miss Rachel!"

"I'm…sorry, honey." Rachel gasped.

"Don't cry, Miss Rachel. I'll be okay! I'm unsinkable, remember?"

More tears gushed down her face at the child's attempt to comfort her. Another volunteer closed the rear doors and thumped on them. The ambulance pulled away. Tom patted her on the shoulder. "She's a tough kid. You want to ride with me to the hospital?"

Unable to speak, Rachel shook her head and sank to the curb, pins and needles assaulting her hands and feet.

"You're hyperventilating," a fireman said. "Breathe slowly. Everything will be all right." The man continued to coach her in slowing her respiration rate.

Everything would be all right?

Then why did she feel as if she'd just failed the most important test of her life?

THE FRONT PORCH LIGHT gleamed, a welcoming beacon as James pulled into the driveway. Exhausted by first the patient's crisis, then dealing with Molly's unexpected trip to the ER, he sat in the SUV for a minute, gathering what was left of his energy reserve to carry his now-sleeping daughter into the house and upstairs to her room.

The front door opened. Rachel stood, silhouetted in the frame. His heart twisted, a heavy sensation settled into his stomach.

He'd done some thinking while in the ER.

A lot of thinking.

And postponing what he'd decided wouldn't make it any easier. For either of them. He slowly climbed from the vehicle, picked Molly up out of the back seat, bumped the door closed with his hip and started up the porch steps.

"How is she?" Rachel whispered. She reached toward Molly, then jammed her hands into her pockets without touching her.

"Her wrist is sprained. They don't think there's a concussion. Three stitches in the forehead, a few bumps and bruises, but she'll be fine. Probably a little sore for a few days.'' James brushed past her and continued through the foyer toward the stairs. ''I'm going to put her to bed, then I'll be back down. We have to talk.''

Did that sound as ominous to her as it did to him? After getting Molly settled and spending too long in a search for the monitor he used when she was sick, he returned to the first floor. Rachel was in the living room, standing near the piano, gazing at the pictures of Molly on the wall. She turned as he entered.

''James, I am so sorry. I tried to stop her.... I feel so horrible about this.''

He lifted one shoulder. ''It was an accident, Rachel. These things happen. I try hard to see that they don't, but sometimes, they do. It wasn't your fault.''

''You are too good to be true, James McClain.'' Her lower lip trembled slightly, and her blue eyes misted over.

A strong urge to take her into his arms swept through him, but he didn't dare. It would only make things harder. ''Rachel—''

''James—'' she said at the same time.

After an awkward silence, they exchanged rueful smiles. ''You go first,'' she said.

Oh, thanks. He fumbled for the right words. ''You know that Molly's my life, Rachel. Ever since she was born, she's been the center of my universe. My life has been defined by being a dad. For a little while, you've managed to remind me of what it means to be a man. For that, I'm tremendously grateful.''

"But?" Her eyebrows drew downward and her shoulders slumped in a silent and unconscious admission that she knew where he was headed.

His own stomach knotted. He didn't want to hurt her, but there was no way around it. "But…tonight I remembered that she has to come first. Rachel, she cried tonight in the hospital, not because she'd been injured, but because she hurt you."

The tears came closer to spilling over, but somehow she managed to contain them. He could almost see the walls going back up around her as he spoke.

The walls he'd worked so hard to help her tear down. He hated himself for causing her more grief. "A few days ago you claimed to love me. But you said it yourself, Rachel. Love is being there for the hard stuff. And tonight, you weren't. And that hurt Molly." *And me.*

And so did this. But he had no choice. His little girl was worth every sacrifice he made for her.

Her lips compressed into a thin, flat line, and she nodded. "I know. Guess we were thinking the same thing. This—" she waved her hands between the two of them "—it isn't fair to her. She wants a new mom. And you both deserve someone who can be there for you. For the hard stuff."

"Yeah."

"I really wish—" her voice broke, and she glanced away "—I wish that could be me."

"God, so do I," he whispered around the huge lump in his throat.

"But wishes and magic aren't enough in the light of real life, are they? Guess it only works in moonlit fantasies and summer romances." She looked back at him. "We probably should have quit while we were ahead, huh?"

"Maybe." Maybe it wouldn't have hurt as much if he'd had the sense to let her go at the end of camp. To keep just those memories. It sure as hell would have been easier for Molly, who now had her heart set on Rachel becoming a permanent part of their family. Which was why he had to end it now. His little girl deserved a mother who could deal with sitting at a hospital bedside.

But he felt like Scrooge and the Grinch all rolled up into one. Suddenly it was as if the magic had been sucked out of the universe.

"My suitcase is already in the Goat."

He nodded, grateful she'd come to the same conclusion. And incredibly saddened. Because it proved even more what a special woman she was. A woman who put the needs of his daughter ahead of her own wants and desires. Or his.

Dammit, life wasn't fair.

"I'll—I'll walk you to the door."

The stillness in the house was broken only by the sound of their shoes on the wooden floor in the foyer. She hesitated in the open doorway, then turned to him. She cupped his face with her hands. Her lips moved but no sound came from them. Finally, she pulled his head down and pressed her mouth to his. The kiss tasted salty…from tears. And to his horror, he realized at least one of them had come from him. He backed away.

"Thank you, James."

"For what?"

"For reminding me that life is for living." She turned and strode across the porch.

"Rachel," he called after her.

She stopped on the top step, but didn't look back.

"Promise me you'll find a counselor." He couldn't bear to think of her going through life with continued panic attacks.

Her head bobbed. "I promise." She squared her shoulders and marched down the stairs, off his porch, and out of his life. He shut the front door ever-so-gently and turned back into the house. She'd been there little more than twenty-four hours.

But she left behind an empty space he could feel.

CHAPTER EIGHTEEN

RACHEL FLIPPED THE PAGES of the teacher's guide, then typed in the numbers for next week's classes. Finished, she printed out the pages and tucked them into her plan book. She stretched and rolled her head to get the kinks out of her neck.

The chairs were upended on their desktops, loaded backpacks on top, ready for dismissal when her students came back from art class.

From a neighboring classroom she could hear a chorus of young voices reading in unison. The silence in her own room was a relief to her aching head.

Although the quiet left her with too much time for reflection, for counting the time since she'd seen James and Molly—four and a half weeks.

But there was no use dwelling on things she couldn't change. With a sigh, she grabbed a stack of papers from the ''to be graded'' box and picked up her red pen. If nothing else, James had helped her get her act together. She'd even started working on her hospital phobia with a counselor. Although she liked her new therapist—a woman—she missed

James's unorthodox methods. Her thoughts were interrupted by the shrill chirp of her cell phone.

"Hello?"

"Rachel?"

She fumbled with the tiny black phone. "James? Is that you?"

"Yeah. It's me."

"It's good to hear from you." And totally unexpected. "How are you?"

A heavy sigh filtered through the phone. "Actually, not very good."

"Oh?" A faint flicker of hope surfaced. Maybe he missed her as much as she did him?

"I'm calling…because Molly insisted." He cleared his throat. "She wanted you to know. She's in the hospital."

Rachel's free hand flew to her mouth. She forced it back down to her lap. "Oh, no! James, what's wrong?"

"She's…" His voice faded out like a fallen leaf blown away. "She's rejecting."

"No! Oh, God, James, I'm so sorry." A long silence stretched between them. "What happened? How did you know she was sick?"

"I didn't. It was supposed to be a routine biopsy. I had no idea anything was wrong."

"What exactly does this mean for her? How do they treat this?"

"With bigger doses of the drugs she normally takes."

"And if that doesn't help?"

The sigh was longer, deeper this time, more like a tightly controlled exhalation. "Then I sit by her bedside and pray for another miracle."

A miracle that means the death of someone else's child, Rachel thought.

"I need..."

"What?"

He hesitated, then said, "Will you call her later? Send her a card, something? She misses you."

Rachel shuffled the papers around on her desk, grabbed her purse and headed for the door. Her "teacher" shoes clattered against the highly polished floor as she strode down the hallway. "Of course, James. You tell her I'll talk to her later, okay?"

"Thanks, Rachel." He breathed loudly again. "I'm outside on my cell. I have to get back to her. You...you take care of yourself, huh?"

"You take care of that little girl."

"I'm doing my best."

A click indicated he'd hung up. Rachel raced into the office, stuffing the phone back into her pocketbook. "Is Jerry in his office?" she asked Camille, the school secretary.

"Yes. Go on in, Rachel."

When she charged in, Jerry glanced up from some paperwork spread across his desk. A tight look of anxiety filled his face. "Rachel? What's wrong?"

"I need you to cover for my kids when they come back from art. All you have to do is dismiss them. And call a sub for me for tomorrow. Probably Friday, too, but I'll let you know that tomorrow."

"Why? What's going on?" He rose from his chair and strode around the desk.

"I've got to go to Pittsburgh. To Children's Hospital. Molly McClain is rejecting her heart."

Jerry cursed softly. "I'm sorry, Rachel. Are you sure you're up to it? It's a long ride by yourself when you're stressed."

"I'm hoping not to go alone. You'll take care of my class for me, right?"

"Absolutely. Keep me posted."

Rachel nodded. On her way out of the building, she dug her cell phone out again. "Dad? It's me, Rae. Listen, I need some help. Can you meet me at my place?" She'd change her clothes and hit the road.

HER HEART STARTED TRIPPING over itself as they walked through the automatic doors. She wiped her hands across her jeans. Her father pressed his fingers to her back, steered her onto the rug in the waiting area. "You can do this," he murmured, going to his knees in front of her.

"What are you doing?" She looked around the lobby to see if anyone was noticing her father's odd behavior. She'd asked him to come with her because she figured she had a better chance of staying strong in front of him. He would accept nothing less from her.

"Tightening your boot laces." He yanked on the strings, deftly retying the black combat boots she kept for field trips to muddy wilderness areas. With a fluid grace, he rose and gripped her forearms, causing the brown paper bag in her hand to rattle. "Feel that in your ankles?"

She nodded.

"Focus on that feeling and nothing else. On your objective. There's a little girl and a man upstairs who need you."

"Yessir."

Awkwardly he pulled her into an embrace. "Courage isn't the absence of fear, Rae," he muttered into her ear. "It's doing what needs to be done even though you're scared shitless. You are a courageous woman who's faced a lot in her life. I'm damn proud of you, girl."

He broke off the hug, laid his hands on her shoulders and spun her around, so she was facing in the direction of the information desk. "Now march, soldier. Head up, shoulders back." He gave her a gentle push forward, then spoke softly, "You can do it. I'll be here, waiting."

Buoyed by her father's unexpected empathy, she moved forward, collecting the visitor's pass from the white-haired woman at the desk. After stopping to wash her hands, she headed for the bank of elevators. Sweat popped out on the back of her neck and across her forehead. She clutched the little bag tighter. It served two purposes: one, it held a gift for Molly, and two, if she needed it, she could treat herself for hyperventilation. With any luck, it wouldn't need to serve as a barf bag.

She strode into the elevator, focusing on the tight boots on her feet and the man and child upstairs who waited for her.

JAMES LEANED OVER and kissed his mother on the cheek as one set of elevator doors opened. "Bye, Mom. Thanks for being here."

"You know I wouldn't be anywhere else. Dad will take the morning shift again tomorrow because I've got a dentist appointment, but I'll be here after lunch. Don't you worry." She boarded the elevator and kept the doors open with one hand, then wagged a well-manicured finger at him. "Be sure to call Michelle. She sounded worried when Cherish called Molly's room earlier while you were out. And make sure you eat some dinner. You don't do her any good when you run yourself ragged."

"Yes, Mom."

"And don't forget, my quilting group is having that auction this weekend for Molly's medical fund."

"I had forgotten. I've kinda got other things on my mind right now. You give the ladies my love and gratitude, okay?"

She nodded and let the doors close, leaving him

alone in the hospital hallway. He crossed to a blue bench against the wall and sank down onto it. Propping his elbows on his knees, he rested his face in his palms. Molly was watching reruns of old television shows in her room, and he needed a few minutes to get himself back together before he returned to her.

He'd screwed up on the phone with Rachel earlier today. For someone preaching honest emotions, he hadn't been very honest with her.

He rubbed his fingertips around his temples. More than anything, he could do with a big dose of her strength, her put-on-a-brave-face-and-march-on attitude.

A clump of people brushed by him, stirring up a breeze. James kept his head down. Another elevator pinged as they got on it.

You can do this. Put on a smile and get in there and face your daughter. Positive thinking, positive speaking, positive outcome.

Lost in his thoughts, he took a moment to realize someone was standing beside him.

Lemons. Damn it all if now he wasn't hallucinating her smell.

James lowered his hands and opened his eyes. A pair of spit-shined black combat boots greeted him. He followed black jeans upward while asking, "Can I help you?"

"I thought maybe I could help you," Rachel said, voice raspy. Her skin gleamed, ghastly pale under the fluorescent lights. A bead of sweat trickled down the edge of her face, and she swiped at it with the back of her trembling hand.

James jumped from the bench. "Rachel!" He clasped his fingers together behind himself, hoping to contain the urge to touch her. "How are you?"

"I've missed you like crazy, I'm worried as hell about Molly, and I feel like I'm gonna puke or pass out. But, other than that, I'm fine." She offered him a quivering smile. "How are *you?*"

"I'm fine," he said, stunned by both her appearance and honest answer instead of her old standby response. The one he'd just used himself.

"Liar. And you don't lie well, counselor."

He took her by the elbow. "Why don't we sit down?"

"Is that like, sit down before you fall down?" She chuckled warily.

"Something like that." The warmth of her beside him was the most welcome thing he'd felt in weeks. "What's with the combat boots?" He pointed to her footwear.

"Those are for courage. Lace up my boots tighter, you know? Carry on like a good soldier. If my dad could lace his boots tighter on broken ankles and carry an injured platoon mate through the jungle, then I can do this."

"And so here you are," he murmured, once again in awe of her, knowing how much she'd accomplished by walking in the front door of the hospital. "You amaze me."

She reached for his hand. "When we talked about love, we said it meant being there in the tough times. I couldn't think of a better way to prove to you that I meant it when I said I loved you."

He gave in to the urge and wrapped his arms around her, drawing her against his chest. The laminated visitor's ID badge clipped to her shirt jabbed him. He nuzzled her hair. "I need you, Rachel. God, how I need you. I can't lose her. Not after all this."

A tear rolled along the bridge of his nose and plopped into her hair. Followed by another. And another. He let himself release the pent-up emotions he'd held in check since Molly's diagnosis just a few days ago.

"You're not going to lose her. She's unsinkable, remember?" Rachel stroked circles on his back. "And if we need another miracle, I will sit at her bedside and pray for one with you. And believe we'll get it."

How long they stood there, arms around each other, James didn't know. But eventually he lifted his head, reluctantly releasing her. "You want to go see her?"

"Of course I do." She fished in her purse, handed him a tissue. "You might want to…uh… wash your face first. Positive attitudes, right?

You don't want her to know you've been crying, do you?''

He turned away to wipe his nose, moved by the mixture of love and compassion he'd seen in her eyes. ''No, I don't.'' He pointed toward the hallway. ''She's just down there, on the left. I think I'll go to the men's room first, then I'll meet you. Okay?''

Rachel nodded. As he walked away, she took a few deep breaths. Then she turned and strode along the corridor.

She hesitated in the door. How did Molly look? What kind of machines was she hooked up to? Blast, she should have asked James all those questions so that she could be prepared.

The bed near the door was empty. Molly lay in the one by the window. The brilliant orange rays of the setting sun overpowered the gloomy fluorescent lights. Rachel squared her shoulders, pasted on a smile and marched across the room, doing her best to ignore the IV pump and beeping heart monitor connected to the child.

''Hi, there,'' she said, waving her hand.

Molly turned from the TV, hazel eyes going wide. ''Miss Rachel? You came!''

''I did. I made it.'' Rachel carefully perched on the edge of the bed.

''I told Dad you would. I knew you could do it.''

That makes one of us. ''I appreciate your faith in

me. I didn't do such a good job the night you fell off the stairs.''

"That was different."

"How?"

"This is…more important." Molly turned away from her, staring at the television.

"What do you mean by that?"

"What's in the bag?"

Rachel glanced at the brown paper bag she'd set by her knee. "Oh, that. Well, I brought that as a present for this special kid I know."

The freckled face lit up. "For me?" She reached for the bag.

"I don't see any other special kids around. Sorry about the wrapping job, but I didn't have much time."

The paper rustled as Molly's hand dipped inside. She pulled out the gift, a firefly Beanie Baby. Her eyes widened, a soft spark glowing in them as she cuddled the toy. "Oh, thank you. I love him."

"I thought maybe we needed a wish or two."

"I'll drink to that," James said, perching on the opposite side of Molly's bed.

"I've already made a wish," Molly said. She gently grasped Rachel's hand, then James's, and laid them on top of each other on her belly.

Warmth infused Rachel's skin where James absentmindedly rubbed with his thumb. "Are you going to tell us about it, Unsinkable?"

When Molly didn't whine about her father's use

of the nickname, a quick jolt of panic raced through Rachel.

"I wished for Miss Rachel to be my new mom 'cause I thought she was fun, Dad, and could do all the mom stuff with me. And she doesn't have a germ obsession."

James made a dismissive noise deep in his throat.

"Anyway, now I know why it's really important to have Miss Rachel in our lives."

The child fell silent, making the sounds from the machinery seem all the louder. Rachel tried to ignore the murmur of nurses in the hallway, the scents of the disinfectants. "Why is that, honey?"

Molly squeezed their hands tighter together. "'Cause I don't want Dad to be alone...if something happens to me."

"Oh, Molly—"

"Don't talk like that, tiger. You're going to be fine."

"Cherish almost died, Dad." Molly turned her attention to Rachel. The uncertainty on the little girl's face twisted something deep in Rachel's chest. "If I go to heaven, do you think I'll see Daniel?"

Rachel swallowed a sob. Untangling her hands from Molly's and disregarding the tubes and wires, she drew the child into a deep embrace. "I love you, Molly."

And she did. Whether they had ten minutes, ten days, ten years, or the rest of Rachel's life, she knew that giving her heart to this child would be worth everything.

Positive attitudes.

"You are not going to die, Molly. You're unsinkable. I believe in firefly wishes, and all of them are going to come true. I wished for your heart to be healthy, and it will be. This is just a little bump in the road, that's all. You wished for a new mom. Well, I can't be a mom without a kid, can I?"

"Are you sure about this, Rachel?" James asked.

"Yes, I'm sure."

"What was your wish, Daddy?"

James wrapped his arms around both of them. "I wished for a kiss. So which of you pretty ladies is going to give it to me?"

His attempt to lighten the mood worked. Their sniffles turned to giggles. Rachel jerked her head in James's direction; she and Molly each took a cheek and placed loud kisses on his face.

"Does this mean we get to keep her, Dad?" Molly asked when he finally drew away.

"Yeah." James nodded. "If she'll stay." His caramel eyes turned to Rachel. In them she could see his love, and his fear. His need. For her. Had she been the one hooked to the monitor, they would have heard the faster beats as her heart swelled with love. She smiled at him and nodded.

Molly sighed and sank back into the pillow. "Good."

James leaned closer to his daughter, accidentally

hitting the TV's volume control. On the screen, Hannibal from reruns of the *A-Team* pronounced, "I love it when a plan comes together."

Molly giggled. "So do I."

NO WHEELIES IN THAT THING. James shook an admonishing finger at them as he leaned on the nurses' station desk.

"Aww, Dad." Molly crossed her arms and slumped lower in the wheelchair.

Rachel flashed him her most angelic grin and tightened her grip on the handles, careful to avoid the ribbons from the balloons fastened there. "Who, me? Would I do a thing like that?"

James's answering smile said he certainly believed so. Then he turned back to the final paperwork for Molly's release. Hard to believe that only three days earlier Rachel had raced to the hospital, fearing the worst, and now, on Saturday afternoon, they were taking Molly home. Her cardiologist was satisfied that the rejection was under control. Though she'd have to visit him more frequently over the next few weeks and months, and be subjected to more tests, things were looking good.

For which Rachel was extremely grateful.

James picked up Molly's small pink suitcase and came over to them. "Okay, you two, let's go."

Once inside the elevator, he slipped his arm around Rachel's waist and pressed a kiss to the top of her head. "How are you doing?" he asked softly.

"Good. And I mean that." She winked at him.

"In case I haven't told you recently, you are an amazing woman, Rachel Thompson," he murmured into her ear. "And I love you."

A pleasant warmth rushed through her. She'd never tire of hearing him say that. "I love you, too."

"And me?" Molly piped up.

Rachel chuckled. "Yes, Molly, and you. I wouldn't want one without the other."

"Cool. You know, Dad and I have a—"

"Molly, shh," James warned. "Not now."

Rachel looked from child to father. Molly wiggled in the wheelchair and grinned at her. James's eyes twinkled.

"What are you guys up to?"

"Nothing," James said.

Molly giggled. "Nothing."

"Why don't I believe that?"

Several hours later, her suspicions were aroused again. At eight o'clock James appeared in the living room archway. "I have to go out for a little bit," he said to Rachel, who was once again snuggled up with Molly on the couch. "Can you hold down the fort for me?"

"Sure. Is it a patient?"

He just smiled. "I'll be back as soon as I can."

"Bye, Dad. See you later," Molly called as he turned to leave.

Rachel narrowed her eyes at the little girl. "Are you going to tell me now what's going on?"

"Nope."

Rachel wiggled her fingers along Molly's ribs, causing her to burst into laughter. "I'll tickle you if you don't tell me."

"No! I'm not telling!"

"Okay. I suppose I'll just have to wait and see."

"Yep. You will."

Three-quarters of an hour later, the front door opened. "Rachel? Molly? Can you come out here, please?"

Molly slipped from the sofa, tugging on Rachel's hand. "Come on."

James stood on the front porch, framed in the doorway. "Out here."

"Okay."

"Sit down, Rachel." James guided her to the top step. Molly sat alongside her, and he sat on the step beneath her. "You ready, tiger?" Molly nodded, and he handed her something.

"Rachel, Molly and I have something we want to say. Go ahead, honey."

Molly held up a small clear cup with plastic wrap on it. Inside, tiny flickering lights indicated fireflies. She unwrapped the container. "Miss Rachel, we wish you would marry us."

Rachel accepted the cup from the child and looked at James.

He nodded. "Look inside."

She lifted it higher and peered through the side as the fireflies crawled to the rim. On the bottom, something sparkled. Something gold. "Oh, James…"

The little insects flew off. "Hey, they're flashing," Molly said.

"They sure are." James looked back at Rachel. "Can we take that as a yes?"

She fished the diamond ring from the cup. "Absolutely. I would love to marry you. Both of you."

"Woo-hoo!" Molly launched herself off the step and flung her arms around Rachel's neck. "That means I can call you mom now, right?"

Rachel cleared her throat, struggled to find her voice. "If it's okay with your dad, sweetie."

"It's definitely okay with me." James took the ring from her tightly clenched palm and slipped it onto her finger. Then he eased onto the top step and sat behind her, taking both her and Molly into his arms. "I hope you liked it," he said. "I worked darn hard for this wish."

Rachel held her hand up, admired the round diamond in the glow from the porch light. "It's beautiful."

His laughter rumbled against her back, sending waves of pleasure through her. "I'm glad, but I wasn't talking about the ring. That was easy. I was talking about finding fireflies in the middle of September.''

"Hey. How did you?''

Molly wiggled backward in her embrace. "Uncle Cord has a friend who's an enta…enta…a bug guy. Dad and I wanted this to be perfect.''

Rachel smiled at both of them. Though a part of her would always miss Daniel, James and Molly had soothed the ache in her heart.

Apparently firefly wishes really did come true.

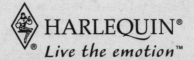

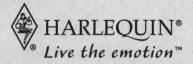

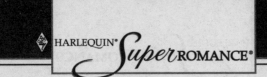

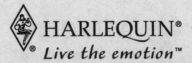